SEA CREATURES PREFER REDHEADS

a Romance Novella from the Phoenix Pictures Vault

BRIANNE GILLEN

Sea Creatures Prefer Redheads: a Romance Novella from the Phoenix Pictures Vault

Copyright © 2022 by Brianne Gillen

All rights reserved. No part of this book may be reproduced in any form or by any electronic or mechanical means, including information storage and retrieval systems, without written permission from the author, except for the use of brief quotations in a book review.

Edited by: Michele Chiappetta of Two Birds Author Services

Cover Illustration by: Yulia Yemelianova

Cover Design by: www.DaybedBooks.com

Print ISBN: 978-1-7372403-4-1

E-book ISBN: 978-1-7372403-5-8

Published by Brianne Gillen

www.briannegillen.com

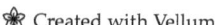 Created with Vellum

For all of us who grew up wishing on stars—
here's to finding some much-needed magic in unexpected places.

Chapter One

Hollywood, California
1947

*O*pal Prince sank her teeth into her bottom lip, valiantly biting back another offer of help. Muffled grunts, along with an occasional rubbery squeak, emanated from behind the curtained-off changing stall in the corner of the fitting room. She had just picked up her pencil and sketchbook as a distraction when a much louder *thunk* drew her attention...immediately followed by a distinct, "Ow."

"Are you sure you don't need any help in there?" Opal asked.

A deep-voiced speaker cleared his throat, sounding embarrassed. "Really, I'm fine. Just got a bit too close to the wall with my elbow, is all."

Opal chuckled. "Okay, if you insist."

She threw a glance at the sculpted head mask on the table to her left. Today was a big day for her. And for that head. Her latest creation, as one of Neptune Pictures' principal specialty makeup artists, was on deck for test still photographs—a sea creature that was a mash-up of human, dolphin, and the kelpies of legend, plus a healthy dose of her own imagination. With plenty of implementation assistance from the sorceresses and sorcerers in wardrobe, she had been preparing *The Kelp-Dweller from Fathoms Below*'s titular character for months, and was particularly proud of her "monster."

Hopefully I'll get proper credit for this one.

Opal shook her head. Working in a place like Neptune had one major drawback—her bosses. The head of makeup, Mort Preston, liked to take credit for the work of his underlings, hers especially. She'd been tempted to make a formal complaint for ages, but it would hardly be worth it. The studio boss was even more of an obnoxious ass than Preston. So she'd gotten used to putting her head down and focusing on her art. Her beloved creatures.

She tenderly ran a finger over her current sketch. It featured the same kelpie from today's fitting, but this sketchbook was meant for her eyes only. A key part of her creative process involved imagining her characters in all manner of situations, not just those specifically outlined in their scripts. It helped her infuse motion—*life*—into these fantastical beings.

But something about this one captured her imagination more than usual.

Her mouth turned up in a small, private smile as she added extra emphasis to the creature's biceps, where his arms curled protectively around—

The curtain rings clanged as her actor pulled the fabric aside and finally emerged. Opal lifted her head to find Adrian Waterson stepping toward her, walking relatively well, considering the fact his bodysuit ended in something more akin to flippers than feet.

"I couldn't quite finish the zipper," he said, extending his arms. "But how do I look?"

Opal closed her sketchbook and stood. "Like you stepped right out of the sea. Almost. How does it feel?"

He shrugged and smiled shyly. "Pretty natural, actually."

"Good."

Adrian's popularity as an actor was on the rise, despite the fact that he tended to keep to himself when the cameras stopped rolling, unlike most of his peers. Opal wasn't sure how the studio higher-ups let him get away with his refusal to court the press.

An astoundingly agile swimmer, Adrian had begun at Neptune as a background and stunt performer, then rose quickly through the ranks to larger, speaking roles. She'd heard rumors lately that they were gearing up to tout him as the "male Esther Williams."

Which was why the studio heads were reluctant to cover his entire head in her creation. They wanted to capitalize on how handsome he was, and she couldn't exactly blame them. He was quite the looker, with his raven-black hair, chiseled jaw, and Cupid's bow lips. But Adrian had lobbied hard for the part—including the full headpiece—so here they were.

"I was starting to worry I'd have to send in a search party for you," Opal joked.

That shy grin flashed again. "You've already worked so hard; I didn't want to add 'actor maintenance' to your plate."

"I wouldn't have minded. Now, let's work on that zipper." She raised her finger and made a circular motion, and he obliged, turning his back to her.

He had fastened the zipper farther than he gave himself credit for. Even so, the suit gaped open at the top, revealing his broad upper back. She shouldn't have been surprised, given his strength in the water, but the sight of those strong, firm muscles captivated her, and she swallowed hard, attempting to rein in her focus and concentrate on the task at hand.

Opal pulled on the zipper, her progress arrested by that very same, damn delectable muscled back. She tugged the two sides of the fabric closer together, stretching them to form a better fit around his shoulder blades, while taking care not to snag the adjacent low-profile fin in the process. Her fingers grazed his unusually cool skin, and her breath hitched when she caught sight of his sprinkling of goosebumps that popped up in response. She blinked and tried her *job* once more, this time succeeding in fully fastening the garment.

"There we go." She stepped back.

Adrian turned, a bit of new color in his cheeks. She wasn't sure if it was a good thing that this odd awareness seemed to be mutual. What little contact they'd had in the past had always been friendly, but she barely knew him. And she had a hard enough time getting people to take her seriously around here—the last thing she needed was to get involved with an actor.

Opal pasted a smile on her face and got back to business. "So, now that it's not hanging open anymore, I'll ask again. How does it feel?"

"Even better." He considered for a moment, shifting his shoulders slightly. "Surprisingly comfortable, actually."

Opal breathed a sigh of relief. "Precisely what I like to hear. Go ahead, move around some more. Try it out."

Adrian's eyes crinkled as he took a couple of steps back and stretched his arms and legs.

A sense of wonder crept into his features. "Remarkable. It doesn't hinder my movements at all." He turned a few times, and then bent at the waist, giving her a full view of his—

Oh. That stretches nicely across his ass, doesn't it?

Before she had a chance to chastise herself for that errant thought, Adrian straightened and faced her again.

"And you said it's seaworthy as well?" he asked.

"Hm? Oh! Yes. Completely waterproof. We have plenty of backups, of course, but you should be able to wear them for all your scenes."

He flashed her a genuinely appreciative smile. "Fantastic work."

"Thanks. We'll see if you still think so once you've got the head on."

"I'm sure I will." He gestured to the table behind her. "Shall we?"

Opal bent to reverently pick up the pinnacle of her creation.

One glance back at him, and she amended her plans. He was quite a bit taller than she was.

Picking up her train of thought, he gestured to the stool she'd vacated earlier. "Perhaps I'd better sit?"

She chuckled. "Probably best if you do."

Once he was in position, she moved to stand behind him, holding the mask above his head. "Here, grab the bottom edge," she directed. "Carefully."

He obeyed, with a gratifying level of caution.

"Now, hold it steady while I…" She guided the pliable headpiece over his scalp, and together they fitted it to his head. If she had a nickel for every shiver she fought the many times their hands brushed in the process, well… *Focus, Opal. Focus.* "Do I feel okay on your face?"

Oh, shit. Any chance he heard "does it" instead of "do I"?

Adrian hummed his assent, so either he had genuinely misheard, or was politely overlooking her slip. Whichever way, Opal refused to look a gift seahorse in the mouth.

She proceeded to fasten the tiny hooks at the back of the neck area to hold the mask in place. At each of her small touches, the fine hairs at the base of his scalp sprang to life alongside more goosebumps.

He had asked, very politely, if he could wear a necklace of his own—a rough-cut amethyst on a leather cord—as part of the ensemble, and since it matched astoundingly well, Opal agreed. She eased it out and laid it atop her creation now, before smoothing the base of the mask onto his shoulders, relieved to see that it blended into his bodysuit even more seamlessly than she'd expected. Once finished, she released the small twist of dark hair she'd clipped up, letting it flow down his neck like a mane.

"All set. You can stand now." She stepped around the stool as he did so, and—

She couldn't help the gasp that escaped her.

He looked down at himself, then back up at her. "Is it all right?" Concern edged his voice.

All right was an understatement. It was...*perfect*. She let her eyes trail slowly from the crown of his head, all the way to his flipper-feet. Even in the room's less-than-ideal lighting, the iridescence of the suit winked between soft gray and dusky purple. The leathery texture of the thick material—very subtly pebbled in sporadic places—molded to his strong arms, and the costume department had added brilliant hints of shading to give the appearance of ridged abdominal muscles. Occasional shimmery accents—almost like scales—dotted the entirety of the suit, with heavier concentrations near his joints. His necklace truly did complete the picture.

And the mask. She had worried that she'd gone too subtle with it, but it was just right. Slits of gills bracketed his neck, and the tips of his ears were slightly pointed, horse-like. She'd left the facial features just human enough that audiences wouldn't quite be sure if they should fear or trust this creature. With the added bonus that he would have enough ease of movement to express himself as an actor.

Her monster stood before her, in the flesh.

She licked her lips, nearly overcome with emotion. Pride, yes. Excitement, certainly. Astonishment at seeing the fantasy of it all made real.

And, deep in her belly, a fast-growing wave of...

"Miss Prince?"

Her eyes snapped to his. "What?"

"Are you all right?"

Opal shook her head. "Yes. Of course. Sorry. Just...taking it all in, I suppose."

"In a good way, I hope?"

She nodded. "Very good."

"I don't know if you can tell in this thing, but I'm smiling back."

Opal laughed at that, thankful he'd broken her reverie. "I can, as a matter of fact." She gestured to the full-length mirror in the corner. "Here, come see for yourself."

Adrian followed her lead, and she was impressed once again at how fluidly he moved in the suit after wearing it only a few minutes. He stopped short, freezing in front of the mirror, his breath catching audibly.

"Oh. Oh my." The raw astonishment in his voice was evident. "How did you…? I can't believe it."

"You saw the early sketches. Does it really look that different than what you'd expected?" Opal asked, curious.

He didn't answer for a moment, clearly lost in thought. He finally shook his head. "No. No, it's only…" He huffed a laugh. "It's something else seeing it in the flesh, is all."

His gaze met hers in the mirror, and she was glad she'd decided to leave the eye sockets of the mask open. Adrian's eyes were a positively lovely shade of violet that could give that new starlet Elizabeth Taylor a run for her money. A shade that coordinated perfectly with his creature costume.

Said eyes were still staring at her in awe. Suspecting the source, she voiced it with a gentle smile. "Hard to tell it's you under there, isn't it?"

Even through the mask, his mouth quirked in wry amusement. "Not exactly." He blinked and his expression cleared. "But as I said, you have done a remarkable job, Miss Prince."

Opal crossed her arms over her chest. "I thought I told you to call me Opal. We are going to be spending quite a bit of time together, getting you in and out of this, remember."

Her sea creature—*ahem*, Adrian—nodded. "Right. Opal. Well done."

"Thank you." A flush crept into her cheeks, and she fought to subdue it. "So, let's get you in front of a camera, shall we?"

Chapter Two

"Cut!"

Adrian braced his arms on the edge of the dock and heaved himself out of the loch. Or rather, the enormous tank on the edge of the Neptune Pictures lot that, through the process of movie magic, would convince audiences they'd traveled to a mysterious northern Atlantic locale.

He subtly shook some of the water off his body as a crew member handed him a towel. He blotted at himself, marveling for the umpteenth time at how much Opal's masterful creation truly felt like a second skin. How unbelievably spot-on she'd been at capturing—

"That was great, Adrian." Roger, the film's director, strode across the dock and clapped him on the shoulder. "We're going to go in closer next. Take ten while we adjust the camera angles. Sorry to say, it's not enough time to ditch the fright face."

"Oh, that's okay. Thanks." Adrian gave him a small nod. He wasn't about to admit how comfortable he was in his mask.

He ambled toward the leaning board set up for him at the edge of the outdoor set, taking in the hustle and bustle surrounding him. Not for the first time, he thanked his lucky stars that he'd found his way to this career. At first, he was simply grateful to swim on a regular basis, but as he moved up from stunt performer to more concrete acting roles, he discovered he enjoyed donning someone else's skin more and more each day.

And his current role? Well, that was beyond his wildest dreams.

He'd never expected to play a character with the very same "fright face" and skin that had been his own, once upon a time. Before the curse that had set him down this path.

Granted, true kelpies like him were more the keepers of sea stories and ambassadors between ocean species, rather than the malevolent predators of human legend. But he still relished this role. Mostly.

As he stepped onto the footboard of his perch, he adjusted the scrap of leather-like fabric around his waist that served as a makeshift loincloth. He shook his head, remembering the censors' insistence that it be added. God forbid anyone be lasciviously tempted by a sea monster's genitalia—or lack thereof in this getup. Though he supposed it was a relief to have the extra protection. His suit *was* pretty tight, and the way things had been going of late, it was only a matter of time until he experienced some ill-timed activity in that region on set.

Adrian settled against his board with a sigh, eyes lighting on the lovely redhead across the tank. Opal. Her vibrant hair was braided into a crown atop her head today, the sunlight hitting it at just the right angle to set it ablaze. The bright greens in her boldly printed blouse further enhanced the effect, and he swallowed another sigh.

At that moment, she raised her head from the notes she'd been intensely scribbling. The second her gaze landed on him, her face brightened into a dazzling smile.

And Adrian's insides melted into a bigger pool of liquid than what he'd just emerged from.

He offered her a little wave before forcing his emotions into submission. He was developing quite a crush, and it was time to nip it in the bud. Yes, Opal was an attractive, charming woman.

But for multiple reasons, acting on his attraction would be a huge mistake. For starters, while his star was in its ascendancy, he'd been in this business long enough to have witnessed how inappropriately a good many men behaved toward the women they worked alongside. He refused to join their ranks.

Plus, he and Opal had settled into a fast friendship in the short time they'd been working together, and he already treasured their connection immensely. He had so few friends in this town as it was, largely out of necessity, and this picture was only prolonging that loneliness.

After only a week of filming, he was acutely aware of the attitudes toward him on set. With the exception of the director—and Opal—everyone gave him a wide berth whenever he was in costume. As if they'd forgotten he was under there, and thought he was really the "monster" they saw.

It shouldn't have stung as much as it did.

Which, of course, led to the primary reason Adrian shouldn't—couldn't—pursue anything more than friendship with Opal. He had nothing to offer anyone in the way of love. Nothing but confusion and revulsion.

He absently fingered the amethyst-like stone hanging from a leather cord around his neck, grateful that Opal liked it enough to let him incorporate it into his costume. He wasn't sure how it would have fit underneath the suit and had absolutely no idea how to explain his reasons for not taking it off.

The sight of his *friend* making her way across the set toward him snapped him out of his brooding. She tended to have that effect on him.

"How's the suit holding up?" Opal greeted him. "Not taking on water, I hope?"

"Still perfectly seaworthy, captain." He raised two webbed fingers to his head in a quick salute.

She smiled as she gave him a once-over, and he tried to fight the warmth flooding him, reminding himself that her perusal was purely professional.

Adrian cleared the amphibious creature lodged in his windpipe. "How did that take look?"

She nodded decisively. "Oh, definitely the money-shot I was hoping for. I think Roger agrees."

They were shooting out of order, so despite this being their sixth day on set, today's scenes would be his character's first appearance in the film. For her sake as much as his own, Adrian was pleased that his measured emergence from the water had the desired impact.

One of the lighting grips bustled in their direction, carrying a coil of wiring. His purposeful stride faltered as he neared, and he shuffled in a wider arc to pass them.

Opal's brow furrowed as she watched him. "I thought I was imagining it the last few days, but they really are avoiding you, aren't they?"

"I am a monster, after all."

She rolled her eyes. "You're an actor. And while I have met a fair number of your lot who are, in fact, monstrous, I do not count you among that set."

He blushed furiously under the cover of his mask. But at least said cover made it easier to steer their conversation back toward levity. "Thanks for the vote of confidence. You know, I'm surprised you're so peeved by their attitude. It's all because of you."

"Me?"

"Mm-hmm." He made a sweeping gesture across his head. "You did your job so expertly that you've fooled even the magic-makers."

It was her turn to blush, and he smiled at the sight.

"Oh. Well, thanks."

He cocked his head, studying Opal. "Come to think of it, shouldn't you be scared of me, too?"

She scoffed, her deep brown eyes twinkling. "Please. Why should I be scared? You're *my* monster."

The possessiveness in her tone—and her gaze—did all kinds

of sparky, fizzy things to his insides.

Yep, loincloth definitely *coming in handy.*

"We're almost ready for you, Mr. Waterson."

The production assistant's call snapped Adrian's head up. He blinked a few times, suddenly aware of the sunlight surrounding them. "Right. Thank you."

"Here, turn your head a bit more." Opal's request resonated far too close to his ear, and all he could do was obey.

She proceeded to lift his mane, still weighed down by his earlier turn in the water, and fiddled with the hooks at his neck. She gently replaced the hair and smoothed the edge of his mask where it hit his shoulder. Her touch warmed his typically cool skin even through the layer of whatever synthetic material his suit was made of.

"Can't have your mask coming loose on the close-up shot, can we?" She grinned at him.

"No, we certainly can't." He pushed off the leaning board and extended his arms, inadvertently gesturing lower than he'd planned. "Anything else need your adjusting? Loincloth okay?" *Oh, fuck.* "I mean...that is...well...I realize that's more a costume thing and..." He trailed off in shame.

Opal bit her lip, clearly fighting her mirth at his expense.

"Oh, go ahead. I'm already embarrassed anyway." Adrian hung his head.

She chuckled. "Stop." She ducked her head to peer up and meet his lowered eyes. "You don't need to be embarrassed."

"Thanks."

"Now. To answer your question." She stepped back and assessed him slowly, head to flipper, her eyes extraordinarily warm. "You look perfect."

His chest swelled. He believed her. He'd believe anything she said.

Wow. Way to be dramatic.

And yet, it was true, despite their relatively short acquaintance. He'd have to unpack that one later.

"Ready to go scare 'em?" Opal asked.

Unable to resist, Adrian flashed her a tooth-bearing grimace and let out a guttural growl. It had his intended effect, and her hearty, husky laugh was music to his ears.

"I think less might be more in this case."

He shrugged. "If you say so."

He could have remained there, sharing a grin with Opal, for the rest of the day. But duty beckoned, and so Adrian headed back to the water, feeling more confident about being a "monster" than he had mere moments earlier.

Chapter Three

*W*ith a frustrated huff, Opal emerged from her beachside cottage, sketchbook and pencil case in hand. She'd changed into her favorite jumpsuit, tied her hair back with a scarf, and left her shoes in the house. She inhaled a cleansing lungful of air and set out for the beach in front of her, ready for a distraction to dispel the lingering effects of an unusually lousy day at work.

She typically headed to her left for her beachside sketching jaunts, but an unknown force pulled her in the opposite direction this time. There was a quiet, broody spot just over a nearby rise that she hadn't explored in ages, and it might serve up some quality inspiration.

Not that she'd needed much of a push to find her muse of late. As she plodded through the sand, she ran her finger lovingly over her private sketchbook, the one she rarely brought to the office. She took pride in every single one of the interesting creatures she'd added to her résumé during her years at Neptune, but her current kelpie hybrid had swum further into her heart than her other monsters. It might have something to do with the artistry she'd achieved with her design.

But she suspected it also had a bit to do with the actor underneath.

Opal had no idea how he managed it, but Adrian infused the so-called monster with unexpected pathos and depth. She didn't understand how anyone could be frightened of him. But then, people so rarely tended to look much deeper than the surface.

Usually, she was ready to leave her creations behind once the cameras started rolling, and her mind moved on to the next one. But she simply couldn't stop inventing new scenarios for Adrian's kelpie. She'd filled a whole second sketchbook with her illustrations…most of which verged on the romantic. And they happened to co-star a woman who looked an awful lot like herself.

But really, who was she to ignore the muse?

Over the weeks they'd been filming, she'd enjoyed every second of the time she and Adrian spent together. The normally quiet, shy actor seemed to come alive when they talked, and she certainly felt more comfortable with him than nearly anyone else she'd met in this business.

Looking at his handsome face didn't hurt, either. But that was neither here nor there. She refused to objectify him.

Her reluctance to admit to her growing attraction to him also stemmed from her indecision over whether his pull was stronger in human or monster form and, well… She'd be taking *that* one to her grave.

Opal let out a breath, hanging her head. Whatever the reason, her affection for this particular monster was fathoms deeper than usual. Which was precisely why the events of her workday, and her ongoing battle with her boss, tasted so sour.

Her toes sank deeper in the toasty sand as she crested the rise. And then struggled to find purchase as she stopped short and nearly tumbled down the other side of the small hill.

A solitary figure sat on an outcropping of rock in the tiny cove. His gray slacks were rolled up above his ankles, bare feet rooted firmly in the sand. His cream shirtsleeves were also rolled to show off a dusting of dark hair over firm, muscled forearms, which rested on his knees as he leaned forward. He had completely unbuttoned his shirtfront, so it billowed out behind him in the cool breeze, revealing the undershirt below. That same draft ruffled his black hair into an exquisitely unruly mess. Despite all of this swirling around him in the air, he remained immobile as a statue, violet gaze trained out to sea.

He was utterly beautiful.

"Adrian," she breathed.

She wasn't sure if she'd been louder than she intended, or if the waves magically carried her voice to him, but his head whipped up and those intense eyes met hers.

His face broke into a breathtaking smile.

"Opal. What are you doing here?"

She held up her book in answer—careful to keep it closed—as she picked her way through the sand toward him. He stood as she reached him, ever the gentleman.

"Ah, always dreaming up new creations, are you?"

"Something like that." She hoped he didn't notice her over-heated cheeks. "I'm sorry, I didn't mean to interrupt you."

He waved absently before shoving his hands in his pockets. "Not at all. I just came out here to have a bit of a think. This is one of my favorite spots for it."

"Is it, really?"

Adrian cocked his head. "Of course. It's so beautiful. Should I not come here?"

She chuckled, gesturing behind her. "No. It's only, I live just on the other side of that dune."

"You're kidding."

"Nope."

He shook his head, eyes wide and luminous. "I can't believe I've never seen you here before."

"I know." Opal lifted one shoulder. "Although I usually head in the other direction, so…"

"What made you come this way today?"

"Just a feeling, I guess."

"Lucky feeling."

They smiled at each other, savoring the moment, until a particularly strong wave crashed against the shore, drawing their attention.

Adrian gestured to the rock he'd vacated. "Would you like to join me?"

"I'd love to."

They settled on the makeshift seat, which comfortably—and rather cozily—fit two.

"Do forgive my appearance," Adrian offered, tugging at his shirttails. "I wasn't expecting to run into anyone."

"I think you look great." His cheeks flushed at that. Because hers were rapidly catching up, she changed the subject. "You sure you don't mind I've crashed your party?"

"Not a bit. There's only so much brooding one should do in a day, after all." He finished with a wink.

Opal grinned. Adrian's soft chuckle rumbled, sending a pleasant vibration down her arm where it brushed his.

"I cannot believe you've been living right here, all this time."

"Well, when a spot is this beautiful…"

He nodded gravely. "Great minds do think alike."

"Damn right."

Their laughter mingled, echoing between the lapping waves. The two of them turned their attention toward the ocean, slipping into a companionable silence. Opal's shoulders relaxed a fraction more with every breath she took, aided by Adrian's buoyant presence at her side. Her earlier work-related anger lingered, but with its edges now dulled, she felt better equipped to face it.

She inhaled a deep pull of salty air, releasing it in a long gust.

After a pause, Adrian spoke. "Is everything all right?"

Opal huffed a laugh. "That obvious, is it?"

"I could feel the weight behind that sigh in my own chest."

His lovely eyes lit with concern. "I know it's none of my business, but if you'd like to talk…"

She gave him a small smile. "Thanks. I had a lousy day at work."

"Oh, that's too bad. Something to do with your next project?"

Opal shook her head. "The current one, as a matter of fact."

"You're joking. But it's been going so well. Hasn't it?"

She drummed her fingers against the sketchbook in her lap. "It has. So well that a few of the bigwigs decided to pop by the makeup department this afternoon. They're thrilled—seems this picture has the potential to curtail some of that less-than-stellar publicity the studio's been getting of late. We've created the Little Sea Monster that Could."

At first, her chest had swelled with pride. She and Adrian had done that. Together. But then…

His brow furrowed. "I don't understand. That sounds like good news."

"It should be." She hummed. "It will be, for you." Unable to keep looking at him, she cast her attention back over the water. "But praise is impossible for my *charming* boss to resist. He swooped in and took full credit."

"For *your* work."

"Mm-hmm."

The angry hiss of his breath fluttered the hair on her arm. "But he had nothing to do with it. I don't think I've met him once, at any of our meetings regarding this film. I'm *your* monster."

Warmth bloomed in her chest.

"I suppose I should be glad he at least applauded me for carrying out the grunt work. It was hard to hear over the roaring in my ears, but I believe the phrase, 'I don't know where I'd be without her,' was thrown around at one point."

"Son of a kraken! How dare that ass!" Adrian shot up from his seat next to her, pacing a few steps before whirling back. "Is there anything you can do?"

"No. Not right now, anyway."

"But surely you can go to the producers...to someone...and set the record straight? Take back the credit you deserve?"

Her smile matched her rueful tone. "Who would I tell? They'd hardly believe some scheming underling over one of their fellow cronies."

"You can't just let it go."

"I don't plan to." Opal shrugged. "But if I'm to have any hope of striking out on my own, at another studio, I need to hold off burning bridges until it's absolutely necessary."

"Oh." Seeming to deflate, Adrian sank back onto his seat beside her. "So...you're planning to leave Neptune?"

His clear disappointment did all kinds of mushy things to her insides. "I don't want to. The thought of starting over somewhere else... It'd hardly be easy. And I do like working at Neptune. The actors are all right." She nudged his arm, drawing a smile out of him. "But I can't take being kept to the shadows much longer. I'm proud of my creations."

"As well you should be. They're brilliant. And the world should know they're yours." He squared his shoulders. "I don't know if it'll make any difference, but I, for one, will shout it from every rooftop I can find that Opal Prince is responsible for my transformation."

"Thank you, Adrian. You do me and Kel proud."

His eyebrows shot up, as did the corners of his mouth. "Kel?"

An embarrassed flush crept up her face. "Oh. Right. I, um... kinda...nicknamed your character Kel. You know, short for kelpie?" She bit her lip.

His smile escalated to full wattage. "I absolutely love that."

She laughed. "I'm glad."

"So you're sure there's nothing I else I can do?"

"Listening to me air my grievances is no small thing, you know." She rested her hand on his knee. "I do feel better, so thank you."

"You're welcome."

He covered her hand with his, and despite his cool skin, she felt heat all the way down to her toes. Adrian's throat worked over a swallow, and he gave her hand a brief squeeze before letting go. As much as she hated to, Opal pulled away from his firm leg muscles. She returned her hand to her book, covering it with her other, in an attempt to trap the feel of his touch.

Chapter Four

*A*drian flattened his palm against his knee, in the precise spot hers had just vacated. He longed to take her hand again, but settled for at least capturing the warmth she'd left behind, as long as he could hold onto it.

"So." Opal's voice came out in a rasp. "How was your day? I hope it was at least better than mine. You looked pretty serious when I got here."

"My day was certainly less eventful than yours." He offered her a reassuring smile. "Took advantage of my day off filming to come out here."

"To think. Before I interrupted, that is." She grimaced.

Adrian bumped her shoulder with his own. "I told you, you're no bother."

"Okay, then… Anything I can help you with?"

"Trying to return the favor?"

"It's only fair." She grinned, and after a pause, prompted, "So…?"

Adrian took in a deep breath. "It's nothing. Some of my usual brooding, is all."

"Funny, I wouldn't have pegged you for much of a brooder."

"You mean my unusually solitary life, which the studio publicists are constantly nagging me to amend, didn't tip you off?"

Opal's quiet, husky huff of amusement nestled squarely in the center of his chest. "I guess not." She leaned toward him, enough for their arms to brush. "Really, though, you may keep to yourself a bit more than most actors I know, but you seem...comfortable with that. Comfortable in your own skin."

A surprised bark of laughter burst out of him. *My own skin...* He shook his head. "Sorry, it's not funny, it's only...I never quite thought of myself that way."

Her hand returned to his, for an all-too-brief moment. "Well, as I said, if there's anything you need to get off your chest, it goes no further than this cove."

"Thanks."

Adrian focused his attention on the churning waves. There was so damn much he couldn't share with anyone, but it would be nice to talk about some of it. To not be quite so alone, even for a few moments.

Especially with this lovely woman, whose friendship—whose very presence—he'd already come to treasure enormously.

Adrian inhaled deeply, filling his chest with the brisk, salty air that felt like home—and blended nicely with the enticing vanilla scent of Opal's perfume. "I've been missing my family of late. Coming out here...it reminds me of them. Sometimes that's a good thing. Other times..."

Her voice was quiet, reverent. "Did you grow up near the ocean?"

"You could say that." His mouth quirked up, though he wasn't sure if he intended it to be a smile or a grimace. "Not this ocean, though. The Atlantic."

"And I take it you don't get back there to visit too often?"

A spike of pressure lodged in his chest. "Never."

"Oh. I'm sorry. Are they...?"

He shook his head. "No. At least not that I know of." He let out a long exhale. "My relationship with my folks is...complicated."

Adrian risked a glance at her. The compassionate interest in her warm brown eyes gave him the courage to continue.

"My parents are both rather...passionate people. They claim they were in love once, but somewhere along the way... I don't know. Maybe they were too alike; their personalities clashed too many times." He shrugged. "Whatever it was, they ended up at each other's throats all the damn time. Jealous. Angry. Sniping constantly." He sighed. "And I fell into the role of peacemaker."

"That can't have been easy for you." Opal reached for his hand, not letting go this time. He flipped his, lacing their fingers together. Savoring the comfort.

"It wasn't. Especially the older I got. Once I started under-standing adult problems, they stopped holding back. Once, for a little while, I had a touch of hope. Truly thought I was getting through to them." He let out a bitter laugh.

"What happened?"

Adrian trained his gaze on their joined hands, more similar than they should have been. He swallowed hard.

"My mother thought my father was unfaithful, never believed him when he swore he wasn't. To this day, I don't know if he was lying. Not that it mattered. She decided to play a nasty trick on him. Finally get 'revenge.' But it backfired, spectacularly. On me."

Opal's grip tightened, but she remained silent, letting him get it out in his own time.

"She hadn't told anyone what she was planning. So I had no idea..." He brought his free hand up and grasped the small stone he wore around his neck. "It was serendipity at its cruelest— wrong place, wrong time. My mother's little prank got me instead of my father. In an instant...my entire life changed."

"Oh, Adrian."

His throat worked over the obstruction there. He'd never spoken about this part of his life to anyone.

"She was remorseful, of course. Devastated, if I'm being honest.

But it was too little, too late." He closed his eyes. "She hadn't thought through the consequences. At all. And the damage was done. She swore if I gave her time, she could fix things, put everything back to rights. But I didn't stay to find out." He opened his eyes again, surprised to find them stinging, and not from the salty sea air.

He risked a brief glance at Opal's compassionate face before continuing. "I'd had enough. I'd given so much to our family, put aside so much of my own...everything...to keep us together. And none of it made any difference. I was furious, and so damned exhausted. And they'd given me no choice. I couldn't stay. So I struck out on my own. Created a brand-new life for myself and never looked back."

His shoulders sagged—due in part to reliving the strain of it all, to mourning the life he'd once had. But to his great surprise, he also felt...*relief*. For the first time since that life-altering moment when he'd initially become human, he'd unburdened himself. Despite the details he needed to omit, he'd shared the essence of his story with Opal.

And it felt rather wonderful.

Feeling the weight of her gaze upon him, he turned his face to her. He didn't realize a tear had escaped his eye, until she reached up and caught it with her thumb.

"I'm so sorry all of that happened to you," she whispered.

"Me too." With hardly any thought, his mouth curved up into a smile. "Though it did lead me here, to this life I have now. So it wasn't all bad."

Opal returned his smile, with a tinge of sadness. "I'm glad for that, at least. But still... You miss them, even after everything."

"Yes. I left behind cousins, friends, a whole life. I can't exactly regret it, but...I do wonder how they're all getting on."

"Would you ever go back?"

A question for the ages. One he'd turned over in his mind on more than one occasion, never getting closer to an answer.

"I'm honestly not sure I can." He shook his head. "It's not that

I refuse to, not really." He could hardly confess the main reason for his not going back, so he focused on another, smaller truth instead.

"I forgave my mother—and my father—long ago. Let go of the anger, for the most part. But I'm not sure I could put myself through all that again. The thought of going back to my role in our family dynamic, repeating the cycle all over again..." He sighed. "But even if I did risk it, it's been a very long time. I have no idea if I'd even be able to look for them."

"Do you think they'd find you? Have they ever tried?"

"I haven't exactly made myself easy to track down."

Opal snorted. "You're a movie star."

"I'm not *that* popular." At her skeptical glance, he relented a bit. "Okay, I do all right. But my family never got to the movies much. And besides, I..."

"Ah. Waterson's a stage name, isn't it?"

He nodded. "It is. Not a very creative one, I admit."

"It's perfect." She hesitated. "And you really believe they've never sought you out? As remorseful as you said your mother was?"

Adrian tore his gaze away from Opal's lovely face, casting his eyes out over the horizon. "Sometimes, on days like this, it's as if...I can almost feel them, watching me." He shook his head. "I know that probably sounds silly."

"Not at all. In spite of all that happened, I'm sure they miss you. I would."

That last was hardly a whisper, but he heard it nonetheless.

"Adrian," she continued, a bit louder. "I hope one day, if you're ready, that you find a way to ease the ache of missing them. For your own heart's peace."

"Thank you, Opal."

They stared at each other for a few lingering moments. The oncoming sunset sparked off of her hair, igniting more shades of red than he'd known existed. And his heart experienced more peace than she could know. Than he'd felt in ages. Unfortunately, the obnoxious screech of a gull pierced their bubble.

Adrian caught sight of Opal's sketchbook, untouched in her lap. "You never did get to your drawing."

She waved a dismissive hand. "Eh, I can sketch anytime."

He inhaled one more lungful of her delightful scent. "Well, I suppose it's getting late. I should probably be heading back." Better to leave now, before he did something foolish, like take her in his arms and kiss her.

If only.

"Yeah. Me too."

Adrian rose, grabbing his shoes on the way up. He offered her his hand. Her fingers gripped his as she stood, sending a sizzle of heat up his arm. He was relieved to note, by her sharp intake of breath, that she felt it too.

He swallowed. "May I walk you home?"

"I'd like that."

He nodded, gesturing for her to lead the way, hesitant to let her go. Knowing he had to, if he was going to find the strength to leave her at her doorstep.

He threw one more glance out to the waves—to the ghosts of his past—before following her.

Chapter Five

*A*n ear-shattering shriek pierced the air. Opal would have been startled, if not for the fact that she'd heard it almost a dozen times already that afternoon.

Yvette Aaron had been cast opposite Adrian for precisely that scream.

The platinum blonde had enormous range, along with a sparkling personality, but the unique and terrified—and, quite frankly, *terrifying*—yelp she'd let out in one of her early films quickly became her signature. Despite typically being cast in damsel-in-distress roles, she didn't seem to mind being pigeon-holed and generally took it in stride. Opal supposed it did keep the actress working steadily, after all.

Yvette had been on the run from Adrian all day while the cameras rolled.

The minute Roger yelled "cut," Yvette made a beeline for the large cup of honey-laced tea set aside for her. Opal followed, ready for a lipstick touch-up before the next take. She wasn't only on set for her monster today.

"I must say," she said as she approached, "I'm glad we're doing this scene outdoors."

"Working on your tan?" Yvette grinned.

Opal shook her head, tapping her ear. "No need for itchy earplugs."

Yvette laughed heartily. "I'm choosing to take that as a compliment."

"You most definitely should."

"My thanks, madam." She took another long sip. "Do you mind if I imbibe a little more before you work your magic?"

"Of course not. Gotta protect those pipes."

"Damn right. And since they're resetting the cameras, I'm going to take full advantage."

As they stood in companionable silence while Yvette wet her whistle, Opal's attention drifted over to Adrian, blotting water off himself several feet away. He caught her eye and gave her a small wave and a bright smile.

Something had shifted, deepened between them, since their talk on the beach a few days prior. Opal had the sense that Adrian didn't talk about his family situation very much, and she was honored he'd trusted her with his story. She also wanted to scoop him up and embrace away the hurt he still plainly carried.

And for her part, while there was nothing Adrian could really do, it felt lovely to have his solidarity over her boss's atrocious behavior.

Yvette's voice pulled Opal back to the present. "You know, you haven't made my job too easy on this picture."

"Me? What have I done?"

Yvette nodded in Adrian's direction. "Did you and the wardrobe people really have to give him such fantastic muscle definition? Between that and those ridiculously soulful eyes of his, how's a girl supposed to act scared all the time?" She pouted. "Don't tell my husband, but that monster's pretty damn dreamy."

Opal chuckled, relieved to know she wasn't alone. "Don't worry, your secret is safe with me. But I refuse to apologize. I like a little ambiguity in my monsters."

Yvette laughed. "Well, you have indeed outdone yourself with this one. It's your best work to date."

"Thanks."

The actress narrowed her eyes. "Speaking of dates... Have you thought about going after Ocean Boy yourself?"

Opal choked on her own air. "What? I...I'm a professional. Of course not."

"Oh, come on." Yvette elbowed her in the arm. "Why the hell not? Let me live vicariously. You're both single; this shoot'll be over in a week or two." She leaned in conspiratorially. "And from what I saw in his last picture, the muscles *under* that suit are just as good."

Opal opened her mouth to respond, unsure whether to admit how tempted she was to heed Yvette's advice. But before she could get a word out, a group of suit-clad figures sauntered onto the edge of the loch set, Mort Preston among them. Her lip curled of its own volition.

Yvette followed her gaze. "Oh, goodie. The riffraff has decided to grace us with their presence." She turned back to Opal. "But why is your boss here? Don't tell me he's checking up on your work."

"More like hogging all the glory," Opal muttered.

"Are you shitting me? Again? That jackass does absolutely nothing himself."

"Hey, don't sell him short. He works hard at inflating his own ego."

They shared a groan.

Opal watched Roger greet the group and lead them over to Adrian, in his sea creature glory. Adrian's polite smile came through his prosthetic enhancements, as everyone exchanged salutations and platitudes. After a few moments of chatting, he turned pointedly toward Preston, and addressed him in a voice that carried to the whole set.

"Forgive me, I know I've seen you around the lot, but I don't believe we've ever actually met. What was your name again?"

A choked snort escaped Opal, and Yvette turned to her with a smirk.

Preston sputtered, until Roger intervened. "Adrian, this is Mort Preston."

"Oh, of course! Silly me." He extended a webbed hand, and when Preston took it, pumped the man's arm vigorously. "You do something in the makeup department, right?"

Preston cleared his throat. "I'm the *head* of makeup, actually."

"Ah, that explains it. Wow, it must be nice to kick your feet up and relax, while the department makes the magic, am I right?" A spark flashed in Adrian's violet eyes, and his mask did a lovely job of twisting his broad smile into something more menacing. "I have to say, I sure am glad you ceded this project to Ms. Prince." He gestured at his suit, while making eye contact with several of the producers. "She outdid herself with this masterpiece. My performance wouldn't be half of what it is without her work."

Opal's cheeks flushed, and she fought the urge to hide behind Yvette.

Adrian clapped his oceanic hands together. "Speaking of my performance, if you gentlemen will excuse me, I have a bit of preparing to do for this next take. It was a pleasure chatting with you all." With a wave, he spun on his heel and retreated to a quiet corner of the set.

Opal pulled Yvette's lipstick out of her apron in an effort to look busy, should any of the group—especially her boss—turn their attention on her in the wake of Adrian's little bout of oratory fireworks. She wasn't sure whether to be grateful for his intervention on her behalf, or mortified that he'd thrust her into the spotlight at the expense of Preston's ego.

She glanced up to find Yvette grinning slyly. "Well. That's the most I've heard that shy boy speak at one time, off-camera at least."

Opal shot her a quelling look and held up the lipstick. Yvette relaxed her mouth as Opal did her job. But the minute she finished blotting her lips on the tissue she'd been handed, the actress's mouth curved again.

"That was quite a lovely speech, you know." She wiggled her

eyebrows. "You really should go after him, doll." She stalked away, ready to scream her way through another take.

But Opal didn't spare her friend another glance. Instead, she focused on the quiet corner where a pair of vibrant amethyst eyes watched her intently. Warmly. He nodded to her, before being called back to inspire Yvette's shrieking.

TWO TAKES LATER, Roger announced that they'd gotten everything they needed for the day, and Yvette could give her vocal cords a much-needed rest. Opal shouldered her kit bag, ready to nab Adrian and help him off with his mask.

But the producers converged at the edge of the artificial dock, ensnaring the poor man in another round of glad-handing. Preston hovered on the periphery of the group, clearly still stung by Adrian's earlier snub.

Opal fought a smirk as she waited for them to finish.

"Ugh, I never know what to do in these situations," Yvette muttered as she drew up next to Opal, gesturing at the little crowd. "I loathe these schmooze-fests, but you never know when they're gonna lead to a nice, juicy role."

"I'm honestly surprised they're monopolizing Adrian this much, especially with him still in costume. You'd think they'd be scared like everyone else."

"Perhaps they see a kindred spirit," Yvette drawled. "In the creature, of course. Not the man beneath."

"Of course."

"Looks like they're wrapping up." Yvette squared her shoulders. "Better get this over with."

Yvette had barely moved toward the suits when Adrian extricated himself from the gathering, and headed in their direction. Preston gave him a brief nod as he passed, before returning his fascination to something in the faux loch next to him.

And then the most beautiful, slow-motion ballet unfolded before Opal's eyes.

Adrian, who had demonstrated near-perfect agility every time he donned his suit, suddenly tripped over his own flippers. He flung out an arm, followed by a hip, to steady himself.

At precisely the right angle to strike Preston square in the back...and send him flying into the water tank.

The man careened into the pool with an enormous splash. Despite the chorus of shouts and gasps that went up among everyone on the set, no one moved for a long moment, unsure what to do.

As Preston spluttered and flailed, Adrian righted himself and sprang into action. "Oh, I am so sorry!" he called out, almost theatrically. He dove neatly into the water, grabbing Preston around the middle and towing him to the edge of the dock.

Roger and a couple of crew members joined the rescue effort, helping haul the man onto dry land, and a studio page ran over with Adrian's spare towels. Preston stood as soon as everyone let him go, grabbing a towel and attacking his face, which had turned a lovely shade of red.

Opal was grateful that Yvette let out a semi-stifled giggle at precisely the same time she did. She'd hate to be caught laughing at her boss. Mostly.

"I'm quite all right. Quite," Preston assured the crowd, trying to squelch his embarrassment.

Adrian picked that moment to gracefully heave himself out of the water. He clapped a hand on Preston's shoulder.

"I am so sorry, Mr. Preston," he gushed. "I'm not usually so clumsy. I don't know what came over me. Must be worn out from today's busy schedule."

"It's fine. I'm fine." He tried to wave Adrian off.

"Please accept my apologies. Are you sure you're all right?"

"Yep. Right as rain." He cleared his throat rather loudly, and glanced around at all of the gawkers surrounding him. "Well. I'll just...dry off now." He turned abruptly and sprinted off the set, dripping all the way.

Roger clapped his hands decisively. "Okay, show's over. Everybody back to work. This equipment's not gonna pack itself up."

Activity resumed all around them—the crew bustled with their equipment, actors peeled off outer layers of their costumes as they exited the set, and the producers edged as far as possible from the loch.

Roger cast an amused glance at Adrian. "You sure caused some extra commotion today."

"I hope I didn't do any lasting damage." Despite his words, he sounded less than chagrined.

"Nah. He'll get over it. Eventually." He chuckled. "But maybe you'd better get out of your monster gear in the safety of your dressing room. Just in case."

"Right." Adrian waved over Roger's shoulder, finally looking at Opal. "Would you mind taking this show on the road?"

"Not a problem. Good idea, in fact." Opal finally unrooted from her spot, gripping her kit bag tighter as she neared them.

"Thanks, Ms. Prince." Roger offered her a brusque nod as he passed her. "You're a gem."

Adrian turned to lead her to his dressing room, but not before she saw it. Quick, subtle. Barely noticeable beneath the brow of his mask. Unmistakable nonetheless.

A wink.

Chapter Six

*O*pal remained quiet, as did Adrian, during the quick walk to his dressing room. A couple of people waved in passing, but for the most part, no one batted an eye at a sea creature and a makeup artist strolling together. Just another typical day on a busy studio lot.

A good thing too, since Opal's mind wouldn't stop churning. Along with her stomach.

She didn't need anyone's comical efforts at chivalry on her behalf. But damn, did it feel good to have a champion.

They reached their destination, and Adrian stepped back to allow her in first. She dropped her bag on the vanity and waited until she'd heard the snick of the door closing before turning to face him.

"I can't believe you did that," she breathed.

Wide, guileless eyes peered out from under his mask. "Did what?"

Opal scowled. "Don't be coy. You know *exactly* what."

The cheekiness of Adrian's grin shone through his currently inhuman features. He crossed his arms and leaned back against the door. "I have to admit, that splash was pretty satisfying."

So satisfying. But that wouldn't help her maintain some degree of composure in the office.

"Yeah, maybe for you. You're not the one who has to go back to her department and face him."

"But you didn't knock him in. You had nothing to do with it, as far as he's concerned." Adrian hesitated, his smile fading. "Right?"

"Well, yes. But I still have to interact with him, have semi-professional conversations with him. Look him in the eye!" She threw up her hands in half-hearted frustration. "How am I supposed to keep a straight face?"

"I didn't think of that." He pushed off the door and took a tentative step toward her. "I'm sorry, Opal. I didn't mean to make your job harder. I was just thinking of everything you'd told me about him, and then there he was by the lake. Making himself such an easy target." He shrugged an elegant, lavender shoulder. "I couldn't resist."

"I understand the temptation." She couldn't help her smile. "And I suppose a handsome matinee idol can get away with more than most."

Adrian bit his lip, clearly stifling a grin of his own. "Especially one as clumsy as I am."

She snorted. "Clumsy, my ass."

He lifted his hands in mock-surrender. "I started out in stunts, after all."

"And it's no wonder they promoted you to leading man. That was quite a performance."

He chuckled. "If you bought it, I'm sure he did, too."

"He was so busy burying his crimson face in that towel, I'm sure it never even crossed his mind to question it." The vivid memory of him, wet and flushed, blazed across her mind, and she couldn't hold in her cackle. "Oh, he was the picture of a drowned rat, wasn't he?"

Adrian's hearty laugh harmonized with hers. "Was he ever! Rest assured, you won't be the only one who can't look Mort

Preston in the eye. There were an awful lot of witnesses impressively holding in their laughs."

"True." She suppressed another giggle. "Oh god, word's probably already spread to the entire lot." A troubling thought occurred to her. "Hey, you don't think you'll actually get any blowback from this, do you?"

"Nah, I'll be fine." He waved a dismissive hand, before casually hooking his thumbs into the waistband of his loincloth. Drawing her attention to all that lovely, monster-y musculature.

Opal licked her suddenly arid lips.

"Besides," he continued, in a heated, honeyed tone, "I don't mind a little trouble. I can't get him fired on your behalf, but if I at least put that smile on your face, it's all worth it."

She drew in a sharp breath. Here he stood, her knight in iridescent, scaly armor. Her sea monster. Regarding her with an intense, molten gaze. She couldn't help herself, didn't want to.

Opal closed the distance between them, took his face in her hands, and sealed her lips to his.

ADRIAN FROZE, unable to believe his luck. This vibrant, gorgeous woman—who he'd been fighting a crush on for weeks—was kissing him. His heart threatened to pound right out of his chest.

Before his brain could catch up and start kissing her back, Opal pulled away, looking up at him with hazy, wide eyes, her lips parted in shock. She parted them further, seemingly on the verge of apology.

That would never do.

Adrian grazed her waist through the webbed hands of his suit, gently pulling her closer. Her dark red lips curved up into a smile that was half-shy, half-sly. He matched it with one of his own—and closed the distance between them to properly kiss her this time.

He tried to brush her mouth slowly at first, but she deepened the kiss immediately. He groaned in response. Thankfully, the rubber of his mask was thin enough, flexible enough, not to hinder his movements as he nipped and sipped at her. The lovely warmth of her lips seared him, even through the material.

Her hands glided up his arms to twine around his neck, and he spread his own, sliding one around and up her back. Adrian tentatively teased the seam of her lips with his tongue, rewarded when she opened to him on a soft sigh. As their tongues grew bolder, sliding and gliding over each other, they both moaned.

She tasted even better than he'd imagined. Like mint and sunshine and magic.

Magic.

Distant alarm bells rang deep in his head. He should stop this before…something. *Huh.* Come to think of it, he couldn't quite remember why he should stop.

Their mouths still fused together, exploring, Opal tightened her grip on his neck. Her fingers wound through his mane of hair, tugging gently. He wanted her to pull more firmly, but knowing her, she wouldn't want to dislodge anything from her creation.

Because he was still wearing her creation.

But what if I'm not?

Several realizations hit him, tugging harder than Opal ever could with her hands, pulling him closer to the edge of his lust-fueled haze.

He was falling hard for Opal. On some level, he supposed he'd known it for some time—since that moment in the fitting room, when he'd first put on the full suit. But now that he had her in his arms…

Kissing had always been a fun pastime, but this, with her, was an entirely different kettle of fish. This kind of fire, it had the power to be life-changing. *Truly* life-changing.

Panic gripped him. Hell, would he know if he'd changed back? Would he feel it sparking through him, like it had the first time?

The minute he stopped this kiss, Opal could find out the truth about him. The truth he kept locked deep inside, that he'd firmly shied away from for years. Was she ready for that?

Was *he*?

As much as it pained him, he needed to end this kiss. Now.

He pried his lips from hers, leaving them both panting. Opal stared up at him dazedly.

Adrian swallowed, desperate to fill the silence, to make a decision about what came next. But words eluded him. He took a little comfort in the fact that a similar dilemma appeared to be taking place behind her eyes.

Her expression softened, and she huffed a laugh. He couldn't help smiling back. "I can't believe I just did that," she whispered.

"Me neither."

Opal glanced down at his mouth, and let out a sudden gasp. "Oh, dammit. I've gotten lipstick all over you." She brushed her fingers lightly—electrically—across his lips, before snapping her hand away and shaking her head as if waking from a dream. "Here, let's get that mask off."

She stepped out of his arms, leaving a profound emptiness in her wake, so it took him a moment to register her words. She had already moved around behind him, and he jolted when she lifted his mane off his neck.

"Will you hand me that clip?" She gestured over his shoulder at the dressing table.

Adrian obeyed her robotically, mounting panic stiffening his joints. All the reasons he'd stopped their kiss in the first place flooded back to him. He gulped around the obstruction in his throat. He wanted to protest, tell her he could handle the mask removal himself. Send her away. Or at least warn her. But instead he remained completely frozen, despite his terror of what Opal was about to uncover.

Before he knew it, she had the artificial hair pinned up and the hooks unclasped. A rush of air hit the back of his neck. Her breath, exhaling in preparation for a scream?

"Grab the front?" Opal asked.

"What? Oh, right." He somehow commanded his arms to move, and gingerly gripped the seam where the mask dipped below his neck, more out of rote habit than any conscious choice.

Opal eased the visage over his head with her typical gentle movements, and he squeezed his eyes shut, bracing for impact. When his head was free of the prosthetic, he let go and allowed her to take it. Adrian held his breath and opened his eyes, meeting his own gaze in the mirror to find...

Dark, wavy hair, bedraggled and somewhat plastered to his scalp after several hours of confinement. Straight nose, full lips, angular jawline. Lightly tanned skin, a bit fairer than usual due to the mask's extra layer of protection during his time in the sun of late.

He was still Adrian Waterson, movie actor.

An intense emotional wave crashed through him, though for the life of him he couldn't tell if it was relief or...disappointment.

He grasped the purple stone around his neck, its weight especially heavy at the moment.

Opal fussed over the mask, rubbing her thumb over the red marks on its lips. A tide of longing hammered his chest, leaving in its wake a wish it was him she touched instead. A pulse of something like anger followed—sudden, hot, and wholly unexpected. Its source remained elusive, hovering on the periphery of his mind.

"This isn't good." Opal's teeth sank firmly in her bottom lip, still swollen from their kiss, as she worked. "It's going to take more than just my finger. I'd better take this with me." She glanced up, meeting his eyes in the mirror. She froze, frowning. "Are you okay?"

Adrian heaved a breath, startled by her renewed attention. "Yes. Of course." He attempted a smile and turned to face her, gesturing at his other head in her hands. "I hope it's not beyond repair."

He also hoped he didn't sound too stilted. Judging by the lingering crease between her brows, he hadn't entirely succeeded.

She hesitated a moment before answering. "I'm fairly sure I can remove the stains. And you can wear the duplicate tomorrow."

She ran a tender hand along the now pliant rubber of the creature's cheek, and a muscle clenched in his own jaw.

Opal inhaled sharply. "But I can't leave this around for anyone else to find." She met his eye squarely, a hint of steel flashing through her expression. "We don't want anyone talking."

Adrian swallowed. "No."

She paused, waiting for him to say more. As if he knew any other words.

Say something. Don't let her leave like this.

He needed another minute to gather the fragments of his thoughts.

But he didn't have another minute. Opal's shoulders sagged—only a minuscule fraction, but he still saw it. He helplessly watched her throat work before she spoke.

"Well. I should be going." She flicked her free wrist at his shoulders. "Do you need help with the zipper?"

"I can manage," he rasped.

A brisk nod, and then she was across the small room, hand on the doorknob. She glanced over her shoulder. "Good night, Adrian."

"Good night, Opal."

The minute the door closed behind her, Adrian slumped forward, bracing his hands on his dressing table. His swirling emotions were at high tide now—chief among them, anger at himself for letting her walk out.

He pulled a deep breath in through his nose and willed himself to examine the maelstrom. He recognized his earlier burst of anger for what it was, the link between it and his disappointment clear.

His anticipatory fright over Opal's reaction was unnecessary.

He hadn't felt any big pulse of magic because there hadn't been one. And he was only now realizing just how much he wanted there to be. With *her*.

He raised his head and focused his miserable attention on his reflection in the mirror.

His feelings for Opal were stronger than he'd let himself admit. That kiss proved it. And yet, here he still was. Exactly the same. *Human.*

Perhaps she didn't feel what he did. But their building connection, the way she dove into his mouth so passionately—after initiating the kiss in the first place—along with her reaction to the sudden chill he'd brought to the room, had him thinking otherwise. He *knew* she felt something for him.

His eyes fell on that blasted hunk of rock around his neck, and his chest deflated.

Whatever this was between him and Opal, it wasn't powerful enough. No matter how much he ached for it to be.

Chapter Seven

*O*pal rubbed at a stray, leftover spot of makeup on her fingernail, buffing it back to its usual red, polished sheen, and completely ignoring her dinner.

During a relentlessly busy day on set, she and Adrian had barely said more than a few words to each other. Even their routine of fixing his mask in place, which had settled into something so comfortable and intimate over the last several weeks, had reverted to a new level of impersonal.

Opal tried not to let that sting.

After fleeing the studio the night before, she'd thrown herself into taking extra care with his mask and the makeup remover. While she had been successful in leaving no trace of her kiss behind, the traces Adrian left on her continued to linger.

Once finished, Opal had placed the mask, resting on a wig head, on her nightstand, and stared at it for an eternity before finally falling asleep.

Now, she absently pushed the spaghetti around on her plate, no closer to figuring out what the hell had flipped the switch inside him the second their lips parted. Had he thought she was all business, jumping in immediately to remedy the lipstick stain? That she hadn't enjoyed every second of exploring his mouth?

Or worse, had he realized she'd kissed him in full monster regalia—and been turned off by the strangeness of *that*?

Either way, her friend and fellow passionate explorer had vanished like a final wisp of fog. And she wanted both sides of him back. Very much.

She pushed back her chair, finally giving in to move on to the chocolate cheesecake waiting in her icebox. A friend of hers had recently turned her on to a marvelous bakery, and while it was in the opposite direction as her cottage from the studio, the cheesecake alone made it worth the trip all the way into Burbank. She especially needed it tonight.

A knock sounded at her front door. Opal groaned. Her sweet relief would have to wait.

She made her way to the door, then froze the minute she opened it.

Adrian hovered nervously on the porch, his cheeks coloring at the sight of her. His tan suede jacket was simultaneously elegant and casual. While his light blue shirt was tucked crisply into his dark slacks, he'd left it open at the collar, and the top edge of his amethyst necklace winked out at her. His black hair was tamed into relative submission, but the edges appeared wet, as if he'd recently showered.

He cradled a lovely explosion of cheerful flowers in his hand.

"Hello." His soft, shy greeting melted her heart several degrees.

"Adrian, hi."

"I'm sorry for dropping by unannounced. I had hoped to ask you to join me for dinner earlier, but you seemed so busy when we wrapped, and then the next thing I knew, you were gone. And I did want to clean up anyway, and pick these up, and I hope I didn't take too long." He bit his lip. "And now I'm probably talking too much."

He was downright adorable. And more like himself again, despite his lingering awkwardness. The relief powering her smile was nearly overwhelming.

"Not at all." Opal gestured behind her. "Would you like to come in?"

The corners of his mouth curved up. "I'd love to, thanks."

She stepped aside to let him in, and the sleeve of his jacket brushed her arm with delightfully soft friction. When she'd closed the door behind them, he held out his hand.

"These are for you."

"Thank you." She took his offering and brought the blooms up for a sniff, mostly to cover the sudden blush heating her cheeks.

After a small pause, they spoke simultaneously. "I hate the way we left things—"

They broke off, both laughing.

"There go those great minds," Adrian said with a chuckle, "thinking alike again."

"I'm glad they are."

"So am I." His Adam's apple bobbed on a swallow. "Opal, I am so sorry for my behavior yesterday."

She couldn't help asking, quietly, "Does that include the kiss, too?"

His eyes blazed. "No. Not that. I…" He exhaled forcefully. "I suppose I panicked. It's hard to explain. A bit of a long, foolish story. But I feel terrible. I've wanted to talk to you all day, but the set was hardly the place for it." He rubbed the back of his neck. "And I thought maybe you wouldn't want to talk to me. But I wanted to at least try. I had to."

"I've spent all day wanting the same." She offered him a small smile. "Funny, isn't it? How much you can miss a person, even when you spend a whole day right in front of them…"

He smiled back, gently. "It really is."

"Let me just put these in some water. Make yourself comfortable."

"Thanks." He shrugged off his jacket and draped it on one of the pegs by the door, before following her into the kitchen.

She had hoped for a moment to catch her breath, but his presence in her cozy kitchen was oddly comforting. He certainly had a talent for warming her bloodstream in multiple ways at once.

Opal busied herself with finding and filling her favorite sea-glass green vase. "Would you like some wine?"

"I'd love some. But you're busy! Please let me pour."

She smiled, unwrapping the flowers. "Okay. Glasses are up there." She nodded at the cabinet in front of him. "And there's an open bottle on the table."

Adrian followed her instructions, pausing when he took in the table, and her sorry spaghetti. "Oh. I hope I didn't interrupt your dinner."

"No, I was mostly finished. About to have dessert, actually." Before he could apologize again, she added, "But I'm glad you're here."

His face brightened. "Me too." He poured his own glass of wine and gestured with the bottle. "May I top you off?"

"Sure, thanks." Opal brought the freshly arranged flowers to the table and gestured him back toward the living room. When they were both settled on the couch, she risked a confession. "I'm happy to know that kiss isn't what you regretted."

Adrian immediately reached out to cover her hand with his. "No, the kiss was wonderful. *You're* wonderful, Opal."

Satisfaction and delight radiated through her body.

Adrian sighed. "I wish I could explain… I suppose I'm still figuring it all out myself." He took a sip of wine and leaned back in his seat, his hand slipping from hers in the process. "It's been quite a while since I've been in any kind of serious relationship. I tend to avoid them."

"Because of everything with your parents?"

"Yeah." He offered her a soft smile. "Kissing you unlocked a lot more than I expected. I realized I've come to feel quite a lot for you, in such a short time. On the heels of that, I started wondering…first, whether you felt the same. Then, if you do, and you saw who I really am, underneath it all…would you still? Even if by some miracle you did, what next? And if it's all as real as I hoped, then why...?" He trailed off, lost in his thoughts, then huffed a slightly bitter laugh, snapping himself out of it. "In other words, I panicked."

It was Opal's turn to envelop his hand. "I do feel the same. And I'm sorry if I gave you the wrong impression by jumping in to fix your mask right away. I guess I was feeling a little over-whelmed too."

He turned his hand over to lace their fingers together. "We're quite the pair, aren't we?"

"We are." She chuckled, before sobering. "But don't sell your-self short, Adrian. You've already shown me so much of yourself, and I'm honored. Impressed too. From where I'm sitting, you have quite a lot to offer."

His eyes brightened. In the waning light slanting through the windows, his necklace held an eerily matching glow.

Opal took a deep breath, not finished yet. She kept her voice quiet, but forceful, when she continued, "Please don't sell me short, either." His grip tightened on hers. "I can handle a lot. Since I sincerely doubt you're a murderer or something equally nefari-ous..." She paused, cocking an eyebrow in question, gratified by his answering negatory head shake. "Then I know what I want. And I want to see where this goes between us. It's not like we have to figure it all out after just one kiss...no matter how lovely."

The rumble in Adrian's chest was part laughter, part sigh of relief. "We do have plenty of time, don't we?" He shook his head, chagrined. "I don't know why I was in such a rush." He met her gaze again, eyes a violet blaze. "And I would like to see where we go, too."

He brought their joined hands to his lips and planted a kiss on hers, and they shared a grin.

"Want some more wine?" Opal asked.

"I'd love some."

She picked up their glasses and stood, but couldn't resist bending back down to brush her lips over his. "Be right back."

Once in the kitchen, Opal took a second to breathe, to savor the warmth building in her chest and fueling the smile that tipped up the corners of her mouth.

While she wished Adrian had simply talked to her about his worries right after their kiss, she understood why he hadn't. Her own fears had propelled her out of his dressing room, rather than pushing or questioning him. They'd been in awfully similar boats all day, but she was glad now that they'd waited, that he was here now, where it was just the two of them.

"You have quite an extraordinary view," Adrian called from the living room.

"I really do." She got to work refilling their wine, eager to get back to him.

She was inordinately relieved that he hadn't thought anything of her kissing him in costume. As her monster. She supposed she shouldn't have worried. He'd always seemed pleased when she referred to the monster as "hers," after all.

Opal continued speaking before she left the kitchen. "I was already enamored with this place. I mean, the bathtub might be the biggest I've ever seen. But when I saw that view, I knew I had to move in. I—"

She froze the minute she stepped into the living room. Adrian stood by the window, in front of her drafting table. Her sketchbook in his hands.

Her private sketchbook.

The one she'd left open on the table, not expecting company.

Oh, no.

drian couldn't believe what he was seeing. Page after page of his sea creature persona, the one she'd nicknamed Kel, and a redhead who bore a striking resemblance to Opal. In all manner of fun scenarios, many of them romantic in nature. The pair of them dancing, going for a swim…embracing. He noticed his own necklace in every single illustration.

It was *marvelous.*

He looked up to find Opal, returned from the kitchen, her face frozen in dawning horror.

"Opal? What's wrong?"

"You…" She gulped, voice barely above a whisper. "You found my sketches."

"I did. The book was open…" *Oh. I've crossed a line by leafing through them, haven't I?* "I'm sorry, I hope you don't mind I looked."

"Yes. I mean, no. I…" She let out a weak laugh. "I, um…I don't show them to too many people. Anyone, really."

"Why? They're beautiful."

"Thank you. But the subject matter…"

He glanced down at said subject matter. He'd paused on an image of the Opal look-alike dipping Kel backward in her arms with a cheeky grin. His smitten face, peppered with her lipstick marks, mooned back up at her. Adrian had only been flipping through the book for a minute, but this sketch was already his favorite.

He grinned at her. "They're wonderful."

Opal blushed. "You don't have to say that. I know how this looks. How embarrassing it is. Why do you think I keep this art here, and not at work?"

He placed the notebook carefully on the table and took a step toward her. "Opal, you have nothing to be embarrassed about."

She scoffed. "I've drawn countless clinches between myself and a sea monster."

Adrian folded his arms across his chest. "Have you forgotten who you're talking to?"

That drew the barest hint of a smile out of her. "Yeah. The man I kissed while he was dressed like a sea monster. And not a man."

As if that's a problem*?*

"Opal." He closed the distance between them and rested his hands on her shoulders. "You have no idea how utterly *perfect* this is."

Here he'd been, terrified of her reaction to who he really was. But she wasn't repulsed by his so-called "monster" form. Quite the opposite.

Adrian took in the little crease between her furrowed brows, the skeptical look on her face. The flush still washing over her cheeks.

It's time to tell Opal the truth. All of it.

A last gasp of trepidation pinged in his chest, immediately followed by a tremendous sense of peace. Of rightness. He could share himself with her. He *needed* to.

"My darling Opal." He rubbed her arms gently. "That sea crea-ture…is who I really am."

A startled, disbelieving laugh bubbled up out of her, before she closed her eyes. "Adrian…"

"I mean it. I didn't grow up near the ocean. I grew up *in* the ocean."

She blinked up at him. He took a step back, inhaled a fortifying breath, and then the words flowed out of him.

"That trick my mother intended to play on my father? It was a curse, of sorts. She cursed him...*me*...into human form. That's why I couldn't stay with them, why I've never returned. Because I look like this. And I will until...until I find...true love."

Opal's eyebrows shot up to her hairline.

"I know. It sounds ridiculous, like something out of a fairy tale. But I swear to you, it is real." He gestured to her sketches. "*That* is my true form. I don't know how you captured it so perfectly, but you did. I was so afraid of what you'd think if you found out the truth, scared that you'd be repulsed."

He began pacing, unable to keep still. "It's why I panicked after our kiss, don't you see? I thought you were about to find out everything, that you'd run screaming. But you wouldn't have, would you? Not that you got the chance either way. I'm still not sure why..." He shook his head. "But that doesn't matter right now. What matters is, you have no reason to be embarrassed, because that's *me*. You saw that, even though I don't look like me."

He ran out of breath, waiting for her reaction.

Opal stared at him blankly for a few moments, and then a soft smile tipped the corners of her mouth. She stepped forward and cupped his cheek, her palm thawing his skin.

"You dear, sweet man," she whispered. "You didn't have to go to such lengths to ease my mind, but thank you. I do feel better."

"Such lengths? I..."

Oh.

She didn't believe him.

Of course she didn't. Why would she? He knew how outlandish it must sound, but that didn't make it any less true. Or lessen the bite of her disbelief.

"Right." He attempted a laugh. "Right. You think I made all that up to ease your mind."

"Well, sure. Didn't you?"

He inhaled, the air sharp and stinging in his nose. "Of course. Yes." He glanced over her shoulder and spotted their wineglasses on the table. He stepped around her, grateful for the lifeline the wine provided.

"Adrian?" He caught the slight movement of her arm out of the corner of his eye, as if she wasn't sure if she should reach for him. "Are you okay?"

"Just fine." He took a healthy swig from his glass, concentrating on the burst of flavor on his tongue in an effort to block out the crushing disappointment flooding his chest.

He'd revealed his deepest secret, his truest self, and she didn't believe him.

Adrian took another sip.

"What if it *were* real?" The whispered words were out of his mouth before he could stop them.

He felt, rather than heard, her approach. He kept his attention on the glass in front of him.

"There's no way it could be." A hint of amusement tinged her voice.

He forced himself to meet her eyes. "But what if it was?"

She cocked her head, brow furrowed. "Adrian, it's…" She paused, studying him. "You…you're being serious."

Adrian nodded.

"But that's not possible."

He couldn't tell if she was trying to convince him or herself, which gave him a sliver of hope.

Opal shook her head and took a step back. "You know as well as I do… The stories we tell, the movies we make…they're an escape. I paint some rubber, you put on a suit, and we craft a fantastical world. But that's what it is, a *fantasy*. We may bring it to some semblance of life, but it's not real. It can't be."

She raised her eyes to his, the question in them clear.

He held her gaze, steady, and watched her chest rise and fall as she took it in. Then voiced a question of his own.

"If it turned out to be, how would you feel? Would you still…?"

"I don't know," she breathed. "I think I would, but…" She shook herself. "But it's just so…"

"Yeah. It is just…so. Um… Forget I said anything, okay?"

He offered her what he hoped was a smile, before turning to brace his hands on the table. Opal rejoined him, catching him under the chin and bringing his head up to meet her gaze.

She held it, and he tried—despite her disbelief—to pour his whole truth into his expression, to hold nothing back from her, while she studied him. Her brown eyes were intent, assessing, and still oh-so-warm. And growing wider the longer she looked at him. She finally sucked in a deep breath, before blinking a few times.

"I…" Opal swallowed. "I believe you…somehow. I think. There's an honesty in you, Adrian. A truth. I can't ignore it. My *heart* can't ignore it." She huffed a laugh. "But the logical part of my brain… Let's just say, it's having a hard time."

That earlier drop of hope in Adrian's chest surged into a tidal wave, and he returned her laugh. "I know."

"Adrian, none of this makes sense, and I don't even know how to start to wrap my mind around it. I'm not entirely sure I ever will. But I want to try. For you."

He nodded. "I get it. I have overwhelmed you, haven't I?" Despite all that hope, he didn't want to push her. It *was* a lot to take in, and she'd need time. He took a reluctant step back. "I should probably head out. Let you have some peace."

"No." Her hand shot out to grab his. "There's an awful lot I don't understand. But one thing I do know?" She smiled shyly at him. "I don't want you to go. Please stay."

Relief crashed into him, so profound he found himself fighting back tears. "Okay. I'll stay as long as you'd like."

Opal nodded. After a moment, she slid her arms around his

waist and tucked her head against his chest. He folded her into his embrace, resting his cheek on her soft, silky hair. She settled into him with a satisfied hum, and he closed his eyes, savoring the moment. Savoring her.

A few peaceful minutes passed. Opal made another small sound, this one sounding an awful lot like a snort.

"So—what? 'True love's kiss' is a real thing?"

He let out his own chuckle. "Supposedly."

She raised her head, brow scrunching in a disgruntled line. "But you look exactly the same. What the hell am I, chopped liver?"

His laugh was heartier now. "I have absolutely no explanation to offer on that front, but let me assure you"—he brushed a finger under her chin—"you are anything but chopped liver, Ms. Prince."

"Nice save," she replied with a grin. She brought her lips up to his for a lovely, languid kiss. When they broke apart, she snuggled against his chest again and squeezed her arms around his middle.

The breath of her whisper coasted through his shirt and onto his skin. "You feel like…"

"Home?" he finished.

She nodded, her tone threaded with awe. "Home."

Adrian felt his own awe—the rightness of it all—tingle through his entire body. Opal Prince did feel like home. More of a home than he'd felt in years, perhaps ever. He tightened his arms around her.

No matter their questions, this was exactly where he belonged.

Chapter Nine

*a*drian wasn't sure how long they remained in each other's embrace. At one point, they started swaying gently, as if dancing, their only music the rhythmic shushing of the waves against the beach outside.

Opal's body felt like heaven, pressed up against his.

He dipped his head to brush his lips across her forehead. Her hands skated up and across his back, tracing a lazy, heated path. He started an exploration of his own, running the fingers of one hand through her ponytail, while his other trailed south over the curve of her hip.

Opal raised her head, and for a moment he mourned the loss of her warmth against his chest. Until he took in her gaze, blazing hot. His lips curved slowly upward, and he caught her answering smile a second before bringing their mouths together.

They made a valiant effort to go slowly, but it didn't take long for desire to get the better of them. Adrian licked into her mouth with abandon, and she met him, stroke-for-stroke. Her fingers found their way into his hair, nails raking his scalp, and he groaned into the contact. He palmed the lush roundness of her ass, setting off a delicious mewl in her throat.

As they continued to plunder each other's mouths, Adrian

found himself wishing he had his former body at his disposal. Specifically, his tongue. While quite similar to his human one in many ways, it was far more sensitive, his tastebuds more pronounced. Not only would his own experience be enhanced; he suspected it could add to Opal's pleasure as well. He longed to explore the effects the extra texture would have on her mouth, her body…everywhere.

Desire surged powerfully through him—but the longing for his old body was surprisingly fleeting. As curious as he was to see what pleasure he could wring from her with it, there was still plenty he could do in this form. He wanted her, so very much, in any body.

All that mattered was that they were here, together.

He deepened the kiss, and she writhed against him for a moment, before pulling back. He didn't have time to mourn the loss of contact when she spoke.

"Please stay."

They were the same words she'd used earlier, their meaning completely different—and crystal clear—now. No way would he refuse her.

"Yes," he rasped.

She smiled, the most seductive thing he'd ever seen, and pulled his head back down to hers. They stumbled a few steps together, before she stopped to tug his shirt from the waistband of his pants. He continued kissing her while she worked her way through his buttons from the bottom upward, and he groaned more with every incandescent skim of her fingers against his skin.

When she reached the top, she planted her hands on his pectoral muscles, and he'd never felt a more perfect touch. She broke the seal of their mouths to glance down with an appreciative smile. He watched in fascination as her hands rose and fell with every heaving breath he took.

Her attention caught on his necklace. "Hmm. So bright."

But before he could register her observation, her hands were on the move again, sliding his shirt over his shoulders. He let her go long enough to pull it the rest of the way off his arms, savoring the hungry look she raked over him once he was through.

He smirked playfully. "It's nothing you haven't seen before."

She shook her head with a laugh. "True." She raised her eyes to his, hunger in full force. "But now I don't have to maintain a professional distance."

Adrian made a slow, slinky step toward her, gratified by the heavy swallow she took in response. He skated his hands over her waist. "Was that hard for you?" He leaned in to nuzzle the spot below her ear. "Maintaining a professional distance?"

Her quiet moan sent a flood of sensation directly to his cock, now impossibly hard.

"You have no idea," she breathed.

Opal splayed her hands across his bare back, the sublime contact eliciting a hiss from him. He flicked his tongue against her neck.

"It's been hard for me too," he whispered against her skin.

"Has it now?" Opal purred, pressing closer.

Hard indeed.

Adrian chuckled. He slid his hands under the hem of her soft sweater, and she gasped. "Mmm… You're a sensitive one, aren't you?"

She responded with a tug on his hair, bringing his head up for a searing kiss. He dug his fingers into her soft curves, but it wasn't enough. He pushed her sweater up and over her head, revealing her exquisite, lace-encased breasts. He cupped one, filling his hand, which she promptly sandwiched between them as she dove in for another kiss.

Impatience steadily growing between them, they backed across the room in earnest. With no idea which direction to proceed, he let her lead him. She reached one arm behind her to wrest a door open, and then they stumbled across the threshold to her bedroom.

Where he froze, his eyes drifting closed with a weary sigh.

"Son of a kraken," he muttered.

"What is it?"

He opened his eyes to meet hers. "I don't have any rubbers with me. I mean, there's still plenty we can do, it's only…"

He trailed off, disappointment rocketing through him. He didn't know how much risk was even possible, given everything, but he was always careful not to take chances. No matter how much he wanted to with Opal.

She smiled up at him, completely unruffled. "Don't worry about it. I have one of my own."

Relief washed over him. "Really?"

Opal nodded. "I'm a firm believer in always being prepared." She brushed a quick kiss against his lips. "Just give me a minute to put it in?"

"Of course. Take as long as you need." He trailed a finger down her cheek. "I'm not going anywhere."

"You better not." She winked and flitted to the bathroom in the corner, closing the door behind her.

Adrian drifted to the edge of the bed and sat, hardly believing his luck. He'd come over simply to apologize, to put their awkwardness behind them. Instead he'd discovered she was, indeed, attracted to his sea creature form—and he'd confessed the truth of his life to her. He still wasn't entirely sure she believed him. Not that he didn't trust her; he did. Only, he understood how impossible it must be for her to comprehend, to find out her imagination was much closer to reality than fantasy.

Regardless, she wanted him. As much as he wanted her. He couldn't explain why he was still human, but he no longer cared.

He'd love her in whatever form he took.

Because he did love her, he realized. It seemed absurdly fast, but he knew beyond a doubt that Opal Prince was one of the best things to ever happen to him. And he'd be a fool to let her go.

The very thought of walking away from her sent a shiver coasting over his entire body.

He'd just toed off his shoes when she emerged from the bathroom, wearing only a silky emerald-green robe. A robe that gaped open to reveal a tantalizing glimpse of those full, gorgeous breasts of hers. His cock strained painfully against the zipper of his trousers. Of course she noticed, her lips curving into a seductive, predatory grin.

Poseidon's beard, this woman is magnificent.

He was all hers.

He rose from the bed as she stalked toward him. She closed the distance, then ran her hand across the ridges of his abdomen. This time, he experienced a bone-deep shudder.

Adrian ran the backs of his fingers down her cheek, reveling at the way she leaned into his touch. He continued tracing a path down her neck, fingertips tingling along with the vibration of Opal's satisfied hum. He slowed his progress when he reached her collarbone, lazily brushing downward over the slope of her chest. Her breath hitched as he trailed one finger between her cleavage and back up along the edge of her robe. He teased his way down over her fiery skin, parting the robe slightly further, until he got to its tied belt.

He wanted desperately to remove the garment, but watching her breathing grow more shallow with every light caress was extraordinarily fun too. He'd just started a return trip to her breasts when her patience ran out. She tugged the belt loose and eased the robe off her shoulders, the silky fabric sliding into a pool at her feet.

Being unable to breathe had never felt so good.

Opal was all soft curves and glowing skin. His very own Venus, come to life—only far more glamorous, what with her dark red nail polish and the evidence of her talents as a makeup artist on her lovely face.

"Fuck, Opal," he whispered.

Her throaty laugh sizzled through him. "That was rather the idea."

He shook his head with a chuckle of his own and reached for her, unable to wait a second longer.

Their mouths crashed together as his hands roamed all over

her. Her skin felt even softer than it looked, and her curves fit his grip perfectly. He cradled her ass while sliding his other hand between them to take one of her breasts. She moaned into his mouth as his thumb found her nipple and started to play.

Opal pressed her lower half against him, fitting herself against his aching erection, still imprisoned in his trousers. She rubbed for a moment, nearly killing him. The pants *needed* to go. Thankfully, she had the same idea, and her hands went to work on his waistband. The last of his clothing hit the floor, and it was her turn to step back and look her fill.

"Fuck, indeed," she murmured.

She started to reach for him, but he couldn't allow it. Not yet. Considering how his body already reacted to her, things would be over in an instant if she got her talented hands on his cock. With a sound that was half-laugh, half-groan, Adrian snaked his arms around her waist and lifted her onto the bed. She landed with a delighted gasp and yanked him down on top of her.

They kissed voraciously as he pressed her body into the mattress with his own. Gods, even just the feel of his cock against her stomach was heaven. He couldn't wait to be inside her.

Adrian reached between them to tease at her entrance. One small graze of her clit had her moaning—and his whole body echoed her shudder.

"So wet for me already," he growled into her neck.

"Need you...now." He tried to continue his ministrations with his fingers, but she shook her head. "Uh-uh. *All* of you."

Opal pushed on his chest, flipping him to his back, and straddled him. He grinned up at her as he gripped her hips. She bit her lip and reached down to grasp his cock, the feel of her hand so perfect he threw his head back into the pillows with a hiss. She chuckled, and Adrian watched her guide him, holding his breath as she eased herself down onto him. When she closed the last inch, finally seated to his hilt, he wasn't sure whose deep, guttural groan was louder.

How does she feel so damn sublime?

She started to move her hips, and he wrapped his arms around her to pull her down for a kiss, wanting inside of her in every way possible.

She broke off, needing air. "Holy shit, Adrian."

"I know."

He thrust up into her, all finesse slipping away. Luckily, she didn't seem to mind. Opal wedged her hands between them, pushing herself up off his chest to ride him more fully. He let out a sound worthy of a sea lion—but didn't care enough to be embarrassed.

As his fingers dug into her upper thighs, he sizzled with over-whelming heat. The usual at the base of his spine, yes, but also... positively *everywhere* throughout his body. He closed his eyes against the tsunami of sensation, feeling freer than he had in years. Maybe ever.

It took him a moment to realize Opal had stopped moving.

He opened his eyes to find her staring down at him, frozen in shock.

"Opal? What's wrong? Are you all right?"

Adrian halted halfway through the process of bringing his hand up to cup her cheek...

Fuck.

His webbed, silvery-violet hand.

Chapter Ten

*I*t's really true.

Opal closed her eyes with a long blink, more than expecting the vision before her to have been a figment of her own runaway, passion-hazed imagination. But no. She was, indeed, straddling her sea monster.

Which meant everything Adrian confessed to her earlier was not only possible, but *real*.

She swallowed hard.

Mere moments ago, she'd been thoroughly enjoying the ride, the feel of him under her, inside of her. They fit together beautifully. Being with him felt like coming home in every way. Her orgasm had been building steadily, faster than she expected, and she'd closed her eyes, chasing her release.

She had the sense that, somehow, Adrian was growing larger with every meeting of their hips, stretching her with magnificent friction. Her hands, braced on his chest, registered a change in the texture of his skin—impossibly pebbled and velvety at the same time—that she vaguely attributed to the sweat building between them, the saltiness always in the air in such close proximity to the ocean.

Except that it wasn't.

Opal had opened her eyes to find Adrian completely transformed.

Well, perhaps not completely. His enchanting eyes remained unchanged.

They were currently fixed on his hand, suspended halfway to her face. He turned it a few times, regarding himself with a stunned expression.

She didn't know what was a greater comfort—his own surprise at this fucking *unbelievable* situation, or the fact that his eyes were still so very clearly...Adrian. But both realizations brought her out of her daze. Slightly.

"You..." She pushed her voice out on a whisper. "It's real."

Her words brought his focus back up to her, his gaze wary and assessing.

"I wanted to believe you," she continued. "I wasn't lying when I said it. But..." She inhaled a ragged breath. "I don't think I really did. Really *could*. Holy shit, Adrian."

The last was an echo of her exact words to him a few minutes ago, lost in the throes of passion. The reminder provoked a clench, deep in her belly. At the slight tensing of her muscles, his cock twitched. Still inside her. They gasped together, the realization bringing them both up short.

"I..." Adrian's voice broke, and he cleared it with a rough rasp. "Do you want to stop?"

He lay frozen beneath her, watching her with such care and concern—and fear. As if he was terrified of her answer. A flood of affection—of *love*—washed over her. He was still every bit the man she'd been falling for over the last several weeks. Hell, he was even *more*.

Desire—and an itch to explore every new inch of him—rocketed through her.

"I don't want to stop." His eyes flared a brighter amethyst, but she wanted to make sure. "Do *you*?"

His chest deflated beneath her hands, his relief palpable. His hand finally completed its journey to cup her cheek. "No, Opal. I don't want to, either."

She leaned into his hand, noting how different it was now. Rougher in some ways. His fingertips in particular drew out an extraordinarily heady sensation against her skin.

Oh, this is going to be fun...

Opal ran her fingers up his forearm, noting how the strange, velvety texture pebbled under her touch. It seemed goosebumps weren't only a human phenomenon. When she got to his hand, she rubbed her cheek against it one last time before drawing it away from her face. She turned his hand over in her grasp, tracing the silky palm with one fingertip.

Adrian shuddered under her attentiveness. Which in turn elicited a gasp from her, given what that vibration did to the part of him still inside her.

She started to move her hips against his again, rediscovering their rhythm. Unable to resist her curiosity, she stopped tracing his hand and brought it to rest on one of her tits, hissing at the contact.

Adrian's lips—now fuller, but still with that Cupid's bow shape —curved into a sly, seductive smile. He took over, slowly sliding his palm over her breast until the webbing between his fingers grazed its peak. A surprised cry burst from her lips at the new contact—the thin, almost leaf-like texture tingling. A satisfied hum rumbled through him, under the hand she'd dropped back down to his chest.

She nearly whined at the loss of contact when he moved again. But then the unique pad of his fingertip found her nipple. Its surface not quite pebbly, not quite suctioned, perhaps more like little fibers? Oh, who the fuck cared! It felt—

She made a positively feral noise.

His chuckle ended in a groan of his own, as she rode him harder. He met her with powerful thrusts.

"Damn, Opal... You feel so good."

His hand started to slip from its rightful place on her tit, and she dug her nails into his wrist to keep him there. He grunt-laughed, sliding his other hand from her hip. "Let's see where else you like my fingers," he panted.

She barely had time to process the words before those magic fingers found a new home. The minute he touched her clit, Opal saw stars. His name exploded from her lips, and with only a few flicks of his finger, she plunged over the cliff and into a deep, mind-numbing abyss of pleasure.

She floated outside her body for a moment that stretched into infinity, before slumping forward onto his chest. His hips jerked and froze beneath her, shuddering into his own release, intriguingly warmer than the rest of him, as it flooded her.

They lay collapsed in a sated, boneless heap for several heart-beats. Opal slowly began to note the world around her again—the quiet rush of the ocean beyond her cottage, the spicy scent of Adrian's cologne, still somehow clinging to his skin. His *grayish-purple* skin, cool under her cheek despite their exertions.

She rolled off his chest and onto her back, blinking up at the ceiling a few times as reality—a reality she'd never imagined possible—coasted over her.

Opal had dreamed her sea creature into life, and he lay beside her. He was *Adrian*.

She turned her head toward him just as he did the same, and they exchanged matching small smiles.

"Hello," he whispered.

"Hi."

"Are you okay?"

"Yeah." Despite the concern in his eyes, which grounded her immensely, she wasn't entirely sure she sounded convincing. "Are you?"

"Sure. Yes." Adrian expelled a puff of air and raised wide violet eyes to her. "Actually, that's a lie. I honestly have no idea."

She let out a startled laugh, relief washing over her. "Oh, it's good to hear you say that. Same here."

Their embarrassed chuckles mingled together. How did one

navigate waters like these, anyway? Opal hadn't a clue, but at least they were in the same boat. Not that Adrian needed a boat...

She shook her head to clear it, at the same moment Adrian let out a strangled snort.

"Damn, I am so glad we used your diaphragm instead of a rubber."

"Oh." Opal smirked. "Afraid you would've broken it, huh?"

"Well, I mean... I'm not being arrogant or anything, it's just..."

His new skin didn't appear capable of blushing, but Opal thought she detected a flush anyway. It was adorable. She turned her body to face him more fully and rested her hand on his chest.

"I know you're not bragging. Fact is, you did feel...bigger... after you changed."

"Did I?" Fascination lurked behind his eyes.

"Yeah. And you're right. The last thing I need is a litter of seahorses parading out of me."

Adrian's bark of laughter echoed around the room. He rolled to his side as well. "Okay, first of all, our kind might be known in your human mythology as 'water horses,' but we are most definitely *not* the same as those little menaces you know as seahorses."

She held up a hand. "My apologies. Menaces, huh?"

"Yes." He nodded seriously. "And second...even if we were like them, that would mean *I* would be the one carrying your so-called litter, so you'd be safe either way," he finished with a smirk.

"Good to know." They shared a laugh, before Opal continued. "All jokes aside, though... Is it actually possible for...?" She gestured between them.

Adrian sobered. "I'm honestly not sure. But I suspect...something is possible." He shrugged one shoulder. "There is some human in our genealogy—many, many generations back. So..."

Opal hummed. "And that would explain the similarities." She couldn't help glancing down to where his cock rested against his thigh. Definitely a bit bigger, perhaps more veined, but similar enough to have fit her nicely. More than nicely. It suddenly twitched, as if aware of her scrutiny. Her eyes flew to his.

Adrian snorted. "Well, you can hardly be surprised, can you? The way you were looking…"

"Of course not. Just impressed at the recovery time."

"I doubt I can manage more than a nudge, but give me a few minutes." He winked.

She chuckled, letting her eyes roam again. As she took all of him in, she sucked in a breath. He was beautifully made. And astonishingly, impossibly similar to the creature she'd created for their film.

A sigh escaped him. "A lot more differences than similarities, hmm?" His voice—which sounded deeper and more liltingly melodic in his new form—was now quiet, resigned almost.

She brought her hand up to caress his cheek, so surprisingly smooth. "You say that like it's a bad thing."

"Isn't it?"

"I've always liked different, myself." She smiled as she trailed her hand down his jaw, but stopped short with a gasp when she reached his neck. His gills.

She sat halfway up, suddenly terrified for him. "Oh my god, can you breathe?"

"What? Of course."

"But…you have gills. Do you need to be in water? Here I am, lazily ogling your prick, and you could be in serious respiratory trouble. What the hell is wrong with me?"

With an amused hum, Adrian sat up. He gently took her face between his hands. She shivered in pleasure, wondering if she'd ever get used to the delightfully different texture of his skin on hers.

"Opal. Stop worrying. I'm fine."

She opened her mouth to protest, but he stopped her with a quick brush of his lips across hers.

"I'm serious, love." He smiled at her. "I'm mammalian in nature, rather than fish. We kelpies might prefer to make our home in the sea, but we *can* survive in both air and water." The slight ridges of his brow furrowed. "Come to think of it, we tend to dry out a bit on land...and it has been a long time for me. I haven't been in this form in ages, but still." He glanced at her bathroom door. "Couldn't hurt to take a shower at some point soon."

He shook his head, his gaze returning to hers. She knew she should say something, but was feeling rather shell-shocked again. She must've looked it too, for his expression softened.

"All that to say, I'm fine." One side of his mouth hitched. "And there is absolutely nothing wrong with ogling my prick. It liked the attention, remember?"

A startled laugh burst from her. "Oh, Adrian. I'm sorry."

"Sorry? Why?"

His face looked seconds from falling, so she rushed to explain. "I didn't really believe it, believe you. Earlier. I mean, I did. But..."

"Believing and actually seeing are two different things, aren't they?"

Opal nodded. A million questions bottlenecked in her mind, and in the end all she could voice was the simplest. And the most loaded.

"How?"

Chapter Eleven

*A*drian took in Opal's wide-eyed expression, astonished at how calm she appeared despite the shock he'd just delivered her. Delivered both of them. But her questions deserved answers. If only he didn't have a slew of them himself. He supposed if he started by addressing hers, he might work his way into answering a few of his.

"How does someone like me exist? Or how did I get here? Or...how did you capture me so perfectly without knowing any of this to be possible, let alone true?"

"Yes."

They both laughed nervously.

"Oh, where to even start?" He settled back down, laying propped on one elbow, hoping she'd join him. Gratified when she did.

"I guess we can leave out the existential explanations for now," she offered, "since I doubt you know any more than I do."

"Fair enough. In terms of how I specifically got here..." He absently fingered his necklace, nestled in its usual place against his chest. "I told you some of it already, about my parents, my mother..."

"The trick she played. So it turned you human?"

Adrian nodded. "It did. I was cursed to remain that way. Until I found…" He started to worry at his bottom lip, but stopped with a wince, forgetting that his teeth were a bit sharper again now.

"Love," Opal whispered.

"Mm-hmm." He was scared to meet her gaze. Obviously, he couldn't hide his own feelings—their proof existed, in all his inhuman glory, for her to plainly see. But he couldn't guarantee his transformation had come about because of something mutual. A more one-sided situation was entirely possible.

"The fairy tales got it right, after all."

"Yep." He tried for a smile. "True love's kiss is legitimate."

She snorted. "Or rather, true love's fuck."

Adrian laughed heartily. Leave it to Opal to ease his spirits.

She laughed along with him. "And here I was earlier, questioning my kissing skills. When all it really took was… Huh." She glanced down at herself. "I've always thought highly of my honeypot, but hot damn. It's *actually* magic."

He nodded sagely. "Certainly felt that way to me. Broken curse or not."

"Thank you, sir." Her eyes heated, but her desire quickly melted into something softer. Yet no less scorching. "You love me," she whispered.

After so many years living with the inclination—and ability—to blush, it was a bit disconcerting not to, despite the storm of his feelings. How odd, readjusting to this body he'd once called home.

"I know we haven't known each other all that long, when you think about it, but…" He raised his eyes to hers. Better to simply be honest. "Yes. I have fallen quite hard for you, Opal."

Her lips curved up, and she reached over to caress his cheek, her palm tender and soothing.

"That's good. Because short acquaintance or not…I love you, too, Adrian."

Relief flooded through him. Along with a tidal wave of joy. They grinned at each other for a long moment.

Opal's hand drifted lower, brushing over the gills on his neck with gentle fascination. Her thumb grazed his necklace, pulling her attention. She lifted the purple stone, examining it.

"You were so relieved when I let you wear this with your costume." She looked at him squarely, full of understanding. "This is what did it, isn't it? What changed you…"

"Yeah. Many of our kind wield magic, and it's much stronger when tethered to physical objects. My mother secretly enchanted this." Memories of that fateful day flooded back to him. "My father barely looked at it when she gave it to him, and she was furious. I suppose I should have suspected, but I didn't. I thought… Gods, I was so naive. As soon as they both left, I don't know what possessed me, but I got it into my head that maybe, if he saw me wearing it, he'd want it after all. At the very least, it might make my mother feel better to know *someone* appreciated it."

"So you put it on, and everything changed?"

"I put it on, and everything changed."

Opal set the pendant carefully back against his chest, running a single finger against its surface. "I assume you couldn't just take it off?"

Adrian shook his head. "No. Believe me, I tried. I yanked, took scissors to the cord, everything."

"What about magic? You said *some* of your kind, and obviously your mother, used it. Can you?"

"I…don't think so. It's usually hereditary, but not everyone ends up with the ability. Granted, sometimes it takes well into adulthood to manifest, but…" He gave a slight shrug. "I never saw any signs in myself. Though I suppose it could still be lurking."

She nodded. "And so, after everything happened, you didn't stay to let your mother help either?"

"No," he answered softly. "I was so angry."

"Hurt too, I imagine."

"Yeah. I didn't have the energy to stay, to hide in a cove somewhere while she figured out what to do." He shrugged. "So I set out on my own. Luckily, our family had a small cache of American dollars stashed away, for our occasional quiet dealings with the human sailors nearby. I took it and ran."

"And the rest is history."

He hummed his assent.

"I know it must have been awfully lonely for you, but…" She bit her lip endearingly. "I am glad you ended up here."

"So am I."

Adrian brought her hand up to kiss it. Opal blinked a few times when his lips lingered on her knuckles, and her eyes widened slightly as she took in his entire body once more.

He held his breath as her attention trailed over him, hoping this wouldn't be the moment she came to her senses and changed her mind. Or started panicking. But instead, he saw only fascination.

"But seriously, how the hell did I get you so right?"

Adrian chuckled. "I've been asking myself the same question since our first full fitting."

"You were awfully composed, considering."

"Don't forget, I had your mask to hide behind. Inside it, I was flipping my flippers."

Opal laughed. She ran a fascinated hand down his chest, eliciting a shiver from deep inside him. "Kel was a total figment of my imagination…" She shook her head. "Except that you're not. You're every bit flesh and blood—" She raised a questioning eyebrow.

He nodded. "I am flesh *and* blood. Among other things."

She continued her slow, tender exploration, her fingers tracing around to his back and over his subtle dorsal fin. Her eyes landed on his upper arm, and she paused, squinting.

"Is that a tattoo?"

He glanced down. "It is. An old friend of mine had an extraordinarily talent, did wondrous things with squid ink. I'd always wanted one, and he obliged." He snickered. "My mother was not amused. Which, of course, added to its appeal."

"Naturally." Opal's hand hovered over the artwork on his arm, barely touching. "Wait a minute. Did you say…squid ink?"

"Sure, what else? Octopus ink doesn't adhere nearly as well." He held up a hand. "And fear not, my friend acted with complete ethics. Our cephalopod brethren are highly respected, their ink only given willingly."

Opal's lips curved in a sweet smile. "I would expect nothing less from you."

He inclined his head, pleased by her faith in him.

"Damn. A tattoo. Why didn't I think of that?" She leaned closer, her hair falling over her shoulder to brush his forearm, sending him into yet more shivers.

"So an oyster shell, huh?" she continued. "Any special reason?"

He kept his shrug small, careful not to dislodge her curious hand. "Simply liked the look of them."

"And…huh. This doesn't quite look like a pearl. Those almost look like veins. Is it some kind of freshwater pearl, rather than one from the ocean?"

"Oh, it's not a pearl, actually. It's an—"

Well, I'll be damned.

Her gaze flew back up to him at his abrupt stop. "What is it?"

"I'd completely forgotten. My tattoo didn't manifest itself in my human form, so I haven't thought about it in years." He swallowed. "It's…an opal."

She drew in a sharp breath, eyes wide. "Are they…common where you're from?"

"No. They're not. At all. They're not found in shells, either." Adrian huffed. "My aunt did a lot of traveling when she was younger, made it her mission to visit every ocean. She brought back lots of trinkets from her explorations. I was fascinated by them, growing up. The opal was always my favorite." He offered her a crooked smile. "Still is, I suppose."

She let out a shaky laugh. "You know, I never set much store in fate."

"Me, neither."

"But now…"

"Seems it had some plans for us, after all," he whispered.

"Yeah."

Opal trailed her slightly stunned gaze over him once more, before her breath whooshed out of her on a sigh and she leaned in to rest her forehead on his chest. His arms closed around her instinctively.

"When I woke up this morning," she murmured against him, "I had *no idea* my day was going to end up like this."

His laugh was a low rumble. "You and me both." He gave her a brief squeeze. "You doing okay?"

Her breasts pushed against his abdomen as she inhaled. "Somehow, I think I am." She raised her head. "How about you? You still feeling all right? Emotionally *and* physically?"

Adrian considered her inquiry for a moment. "Yeah. I think so. I mean…" He hesitated. "I don't know what happens now, and there's the whole work situation to contend with, but…"

"Daylight is much better for thinking ahead anyway."

"It really is."

They shared a smile. Opal nestled closer, the shift bringing her into more direct contact with his groin.

The breath of her laughter teased at his gills, tickling his neck. "Your tattoo isn't the only thing I got wrong." She slid her leg slowly against his cock, and he hissed at the electric sensation. "I am sorry for leaving *this* out."

He hummed as he skimmed his hand over her hip, gratified by the trail of goosebumps he left behind on her soft skin. "You did have the censors to contend with."

She snorted. "Can you imagine their faces if I'd actually tried to make you anatomically correct?"

"They'd have insisted you put me in a full diving suit, logic be damned."

"They would've." Her eyes darkened with desire, and her hand embarked on an exploration. "But in truth, that little loin-cloth would hardly be sufficient now."

He flashed her a predatory grin. "That's not a problem, is it?"

Opal closed her hand firmly around his cock, and he outright groaned this time. "Oh, 'problem' is most definitely *not* the word I'd use."

Unable to wait a second longer, Adrian rolled on top of her, delving into her delicious mouth for a kiss. Opal was absolutely right. Thinking ahead could hold off until the morning.

Chapter Twelve

*O*pal stared at the percolator on her kitchen counter, willing it to hurry up.

After devouring each other once more—which included Adrian putting those textured fingertips to *excellent* use—they'd collapsed in exhaustion, of both body and mind. Opal had drifted off to sleep against his cool, lightly pebbled chest, somewhat convinced she was already dreaming.

Morning had brought with it the return of her shock. His, too. Despite the heights of pleasure they'd discovered the night before, they greeted each other shyly. All their new realities came rushing back.

Adrian seemed a touch unsteady in his new, albeit former, body, as if there were more than a few things he needed to relearn about himself. As great as her astonishment was, she couldn't even imagine what he must be going through. He'd thought it a good idea to get himself into some water, heading to her bathroom to shower.

He offered her an invitation to join him, but Opal declined, making her way to the kitchen instead. Her decision was due in large part to her desire to give him a little time alone to sort through his thoughts.

Plus, he might need some water, but she *really* needed some coffee.

When the pot finally finished working its magic, she gratefully poured herself a mug and added a generous helping of cream. The first sip felt like roasty heaven.

Opal made her way to the picture window in her living room. Her eyes fell on her sketchbook, still open where Adrian had left it last night, before upending her entire world. She smiled softly. Most of that upending felt pretty good, actually.

Her wildest dream—and she did mean *wild*—had come true.

She raised her gaze to the waves, glittering diamond-like in the sunshine, as they crashed against the shoreline outside. Not everyone might agree, but given how vast and mysterious the oceans were, it hardly seemed far-fetched to her at all that the existence of someone like Adrian was possible.

That they were somehow fated to find each other? The sensation was heady indeed. Wholly unexpected, definitely a bit unbelievable…but most assuredly intoxicating.

Opal sighed.

That brought her back to the thought foremost in her mind in the light of day. The one that troubled her.

Where the hell do we go from here?

Despite everything they'd talked about the previous night, that particular topic hadn't come up. Between the basic logistics of how any of it came to be, Opal's fascination and desire to explore this new side of Adrian, and the revelation of their feelings for one another—not to mention the physical pleasure they'd wrought from each other—it was no wonder sleep had come for them.

But that one specific question loomed large this morning. Leaving Opal wary of just how complicated the answer might be.

The sound of her bedroom door opening pulled her attention back to the present. She turned to find Adrian, in all his lustrous purple, stark-naked glory, hovering in the doorway. He smiled, and her heart melted.

"Hi," she breathed. "Did you have a nice shower?"

"I did. It was perfect. Thank you." He absently scratched at the skin below his tattoo. "And you weren't kidding about that bathtub. It's huge."

"Right? I can never decide if that, or this view, is the best part of this place."

"Given that the bathroom has a similar view, I'm inclined to vote for the tub." His grin turned lopsided—along with her stomach.

"Very good point." Her eyes drifted down over his body, and a vivid image of the two of them sharing said tub warmed her far more than her coffee had. "Coffee. Would you like some coffee?" She paused. "Come to think of it, can you drink coffee now?"

Adrian opened his mouth to respond, then immediately paused to think about it. "That's a good question. I tried some human food on occasion…before… But I wonder if it would still taste the same?" He shrugged. "Only one way to find out, I guess."

"Exactly." She snuck one more glance at his impressive anatomy, with his iridescent bits shimmering even more in the light of day, before making a beeline for the kitchen.

He followed, stopping to lean his tall, graceful—still naked— form against the doorframe. She barely kept from sloshing hot coffee everywhere as she handed him his mug.

Adrian inhaled a careful sniff. "Smells the same." He took a slow sip, holding the liquid in his mouth for a moment before swallowing. And grimacing.

"That bad, huh?"

"Not bad, per se, just…not as good as it was yesterday." He huffed. "Only yesterday." He shook his head. "But one thing's for sure. It's too hot. I might have to switch to iced."

Opal stepped closer and rested her hand on the slope of his shoulder. "I've always noticed your skin was on the cool side, even before. But you're more so now. I wonder if that has anything to do with it."

"Probably."

Despite his surface, his eyes were plenty searing. Opal let her hand linger, her own gaze wandering lower yet again. She withdrew her arm and took a giant step back, squeezing her eyes shut.

"Okay, you need to cover up," she rushed out.

"Oh. Right. I understand."

Her eyelids popped open at the disappointment in his voice, and she surged into motion. She set her coffee cup on the counter and reached up to cradle his face in her hands.

"Adrian, I don't think you do." She flashed him what she hoped was a reassuring smile. "As we firmly established last night, I am quite easily distracted by you. *All* of you. But as much as I'd like to jump your bones, we probably can't simply ravish each other all day. At the very least, I need to eat some breakfast."

Adrian's cheeks curved under her hands as he grinned. "So I need to put some pants on to protect my virtue."

"Yes, please."

"Okay, then." He ducked his head to brush a kiss over her lips. "Be back in a flash."

Opal pulled a few ice cubes from the freezer drawer in her refrigerator and dropped them into Adrian's mug, before bringing their coffees into the living room. She was smiling into her cup when Adrian poked his head out of the bedroom door.

"So...small problem."

"What's wrong?"

He rubbed the back of his neck, adorably embarrassed. "My body...isn't exactly cut out for regular human clothing anymore. I can't get my feet all the way through my pants legs. And even if I could..." He raised sheepish eyes to hers. "I'm not sure they'd fit everywhere else, either."

"Oh. I hadn't thought of that."

"Neither had I. Could I perhaps borrow a dry towel?"

"Of course." She startled into action. "There are some in the cabinet right outside the bathroom."

Adrian stepped back to let Opal through the doorway, and the brush of his arm against hers, even through her robe, sent a delicious shiver through her. In her distraction, she pulled open the wrong drawer.

She sent him a grin over her shoulder. "I do also have a beach sarong, if you'd prefer."

He returned a cheeky smile. "That depends on the color. Will it clash with my skin tone?"

Opal laughed, pulling out the bright blue and white garment in jest. "I don't know, I think it might work."

"Oh, that should be just fine." He extended a hand.

"Wait, you're serious?"

"Sure, why not?"

"Wouldn't you prefer a towel?"

"I would not." He gently tugged the sarong from her grasp. "Besides, this will probably provide more coverage." His expression turned sly. "After all, we have to keep your temptation in check."

She shook her head at him. "Scoundrel."

"You know it." He chuckled as he wrapped the fabric around his waist, knotting it rather artfully at his side. When he finished, he held his arms out, ready for inspection. "What do you think?"

"Dottie Lamour can eat her heart out."

"Excellent." He held his hand out to her, sobering slightly. "Shall we get some food in you?"

She slipped her hand into his webbed grip with a nod. "Let's."

ADRIAN LED Opal back out to the kitchen, taking comfort in the feel of her hand in his. He'd donned the bright, silly sarong in an effort to keep the mood light—and to calm his nerves. He was riding a roller coaster of emotions this morning.

As heavenly as his shower had felt, it was more of an adjustment than he'd expected, getting used to his original form. He supposed it was only to be expected after nearly a decade spent as a human, but that didn't make it any less disconcerting. Even under the shower spray, breathing through his gills gave him an odd head rush. He had to keep reminding himself he didn't have to work as hard to take in air.

And of course, there was the looming question of what in Poseidon's depths happened now. His momentary—unfounded—panic over Opal's desire to cover him up hadn't helped. But as he watched her bustle around the kitchen, he tried to focus on the positives. He loved her. And miracles did exist, because she loved him, too.

He picked up his coffee mug, willing to give it another try, but stopped when he noticed something floating inside. His gaze snapped back up to Opal.

"Did you put ice in my coffee?"

A hint of color bloomed on her cheeks, and she shrugged.

"Thanks." Her small touch of kindness squeezed his heart, and his trepidation melted faster than the ice in his cup.

"So," she began, "I hate to ask, but…"

"What now?"

Opal nodded.

"Honestly, I have no idea." He took a tentative sip. Definitely better now that it wasn't so hot. "All I want to do is take you on a proper date. But that might be a little tricky."

"We could try Trader Vic's. You're certainly dressed for it." She winked cheekily.

He reflexively attempted to raise an eyebrow, dimly noting that he seemed no longer able to raise only one at a time. That was too bad. "I suppose if we go late enough, there's a chance everyone'll be so hammered they won't bat an eye."

"There you go. Silver lining."

He sighed, sobering again. "I don't know if my mother ever thought through what would happen when the curse was eventually broken." His mouth twisted in a grimace, thinking about how vicious his parents' fighting had become by the end. "The old optimist in me hopes she wanted my father to fall back in love with her, having learned his lesson. But I'm more convinced she planned for him to suffer if he fell in love with a human."

"And then turned back, making it damn near impossible for them to be together," Opal finished quietly.

"It's part of the reason I've avoided serious relationships all this time. If I didn't get emotionally attached, there was no chance I'd have to face that kind of decision." He trailed his finger gently down her cheek. "And then you came along, my darling Opal."

Her skin heated under his touch, the sensation heightened against the newly sensitive pad of his finger. He lowered his lips to hers, relishing the feel of her, the taste of her. Attempting to pour everything he could into the kiss.

He broke off, leaving them both panting a bit. "I know it's a bit late to be asking this, but you're truly still attracted to me in my new form? You weren't just saying that to make me feel better?"

She grinned, skating her hand down his chest. He shivered. "I would never lie to you about that."

"Good." He sighed through his gills, the accompanying whisper-like whoosh at once startling and familiar to him. "But all attraction aside. I wish I had more...everything...to offer you, Opal."

The thought of causing her any kind of difficulty pained him. The possibility of giving her up, of losing her, speared him with anguish.

"Adrian." Her fingers nudged his chin. "Look at me."

He obeyed, and found her smiling softly.

"First of all, you've been back to being a kelpie for all of twelve hours. Come to think of it, *are* you a kelpie? Is there something else I should call you?"

"No, we do refer to ourselves as kelpies, though we're not what your human legends have made us out to be, and we certainly don't make a habit of luring unsuspecting humans into our underwater lairs." At her saucy raised eyebrow, he smiled. "Our current situation notwithstanding."

"Okay, then. But don't forget, said situation is still brand new. All of it. Your transformation, this magic—literal and figurative—between us." She cupped his cheek. "As wild as it is, we're both pretty smart, if I do say so myself. We can figure it out."

"We can." He covered her hand with his and placed a kiss on her palm. "Together."

"Together." She shrugged. "And thankfully, it's the weekend, so we don't have to be back at work till Monday."

His newfound relief fizzled right out of him. "Oh, shit. I've been attempting to forget all about work." He looked down at himself. Opal pressed a silencing hand to his lips before he started rambling in panic.

"Stop panicking. Fate's actually on our side with this one, remember? Because of my genius"—his mouth curved into a grin against her fingertips—"you already spend most of your time on set like this. Granted, getting you there might be a bit of a challenge…" She shrugged. "But we'll find a way."

"I will happily entrust myself to you and your genius."

He couldn't resist another taste of her warm, soft lips. Unsurprisingly, one taste was hardly enough, and before long, they'd both forgotten all about Opal's breakfast plans.

Chapter Thirteen

*T*hey spent most of the weekend alternately laughing together and ravishing each other—or laughing while they ravished.

Opal had never spent a more enjoyable couple of days.

In between their fun escapades, they shared stories of their childhood exploits, his underwater, hers on dry land. Adrian opened up about the details of his journey to Hollywood—how he'd managed to befriend a local couple in the New England fishing village where he'd washed up after his transformation, who got him his first job waiting tables while he adjusted to his new life. And then he'd crossed the country to answer that fateful ad for stunt performers who could swim.

Late Sunday morning, they were thrilled to discover that Opal's luxuriously large bathtub could, indeed, fit both of them. They sat facing each other, legs tangled together under the suds. He looked so at home in any kind of water, and it delighted her immensely to share it with him.

Her curiosity apparently bottomless, she voiced another topic she'd been wondering about. "So, almost ten years as a human. That would include the war."

Adrian nodded. "It did."

"I remember seeing you at the Canteen a few times. I assume you didn't serve...for obvious reasons?"

"Yeah. As much as I wanted to enlist, I was not eager to attempt the physical exam. I looked human on the outside, but who knows what that blood test would've shown." He widened his eyes in mock horror.

"Maybe they would've assumed you were an experiment like Captain America," she joked.

"I figured it was better not to take the chance. I'd prefer to avoid actually becoming an experiment."

She nodded sagely. "Fair enough."

"I focused on work with the U.S.O. instead. I hated lying and telling everyone I was 4-F, but better that than the truth."

Opal narrowed her eyes, ready to start guessing.

His lips curved in a sly smile, intuiting her scheme. "Chronic swimmer's ear."

She grinned back. "Very believable."

"I thought so."

"And..." She paused, not sure how to ask. "Do you know how your people fared? With the submarines and all?"

His gills flexed. "I did wonder. But our magic is largely used for protective purposes and is rather strong when needed. We've shielded other marine life from human conflict for centuries, so this should've been no different."

"That's good."

He nodded, and they lapsed into another of their companionable silences, the water in the tub lapping gently around them. At one point, Adrian reached up to absently scratch at his chest, drawing her attention to the necklace he still wore.

Her curiosity sizzled, but she hesitated again, this time unsure if she wanted to know the answer.

"What is it?" he asked.

"Nothing, really. I was just wondering..." She sat forward, leaning across the water to run her fingers over the cool surface of the purple stone. "Do you think you'd be able to take it off, now that we broke the curse?"

His own hand brushed both her fingers and the necklace. "It's possible." His voice lowered to a low rasp. "I haven't wanted to try."

"Why not?"

He lifted one shoulder. "I guess I'm worried the change will really be permanent then. No going back."

She trailed her hand down to rest over his heart. "So, you might want to be human again."

He gave her a small nod. "I might." His violet eyes burned brighter. "If there's even a chance...I'm not willing to give that up yet. And I worry that if I take this off, I will be." He emitted a noise that was half-sigh, half-groan. "For the first time, I'm wondering if I should've put my anger aside long enough to ask my mother a few questions, instead of running off half-cocked and completely in the dark."

"Don't sell yourself short. Even in your human form, you were a lot more than half-cocked." She winked.

Adrian's laugh quickly melted into a rumble, deep in his chest, that was all heat. "Was I?"

She could only manage a nod, as he prowled toward her through the tiny expanse of water between them. She leaned against the back of the tub, his sleek body hovering close. He stopped when his lips were a scant inch from hers.

"And now?" he growled.

His voice sent a pulse of pure pleasure directly to her core. She slid a hand under the water, relishing the feel of his growing arousal—and his resulting hiss at her slightest touch.

Opal was ready with a seductive quip, but Adrian's mouth slanted against hers, swallowing it before she could get a sound out. She met his tongue in an instant, loving the slight difference between them. Desperate, not for the first time, to find out how his would feel elsewhere. For all they'd done in the previous two days, they hadn't gotten around to pleasuring each other that way yet.

Adrian blazed a trail of kisses down her throat and across the tops of her breasts. He cupped one, bringing it up to float on the surface of the water while he devoured it. Her head fell back against the rim of the bath on a moan. Far too quickly, he abandoned his position, leaving her nipple to pebble almost painfully in the suddenly cold air. He slid her down just enough to submerge her breasts again, running a tender hand quickly over her nipple in atonement.

And then his head dipped below the water, his mouth whispering across her abdomen. Feeling his continued path downward, she realized with a shiver that their great minds had been thinking alike once more.

Adrian ran the flat of his tongue in a slow slide over the length of her slit, and she arched her back off the tub wall with a cry.

Holy hell. If one simple lick feels that good…

She felt rather than heard his chuckle against her core, a little trail of air bubbles breaching the surface in its wake. *Oh, no.*

"Wait a minute!" Opal tugged at the sleek mane of his dark hair, trying to pull him up. "Adrian, you can't."

His head popped up again, eyes concerned. "Do you not like…?"

"No, it's not that. Believe me, I *like*." She bit her lip. "But…you won't be able to breathe."

The fire returned to his gaze, blazing hotter than ever. His laugh was practically a purr, the slow, upward curve of his lips near-diabolical. It was easily the sexiest thing she'd ever witnessed.

"My darling Opal." His hands covered hers, sliding them down to his neck. "You've forgotten about these."

"*Oh.*" She huffed, rueful. "See, I lose all sense around you."

He hummed with smug satisfaction. "Rather a wondrous thing, these gills of mine." He leaned closer, nuzzling her breasts again, where they bobbed on the water. "Do you know, they allow me to be submerged for quite some time." He stilled, those smoldering purple eyes spearing her in place. "As a matter of fact…" He flicked his tongue between her breasts. "…I've gone *days* without surfacing."

She gulped.

Adrian slowly lowered his head, holding eye contact until the last possible second when he sank completely below the surface. Opal held her breath, waiting…*wanting*. When his glorious mouth descended on her, all capacity for thought left her entirely.

Who needs sense anyway?

He started slowly, sliding and kissing, taking his sweet time to get to her desired destination, using that extra roughness on his tongue to delicious, teasing advantage. He circled closer, still evading, until she thought she'd go mad.

He planted a kiss on the inside of her thigh, and when she moaned, he added a small nip with his surprisingly sharp teeth. At her gasp, he licked over the spot, sending an even greater thrill flooding through her.

Opal dug her fingernails into his scalp. "Adrian, please."

He rumbled as he nuzzled her thigh, laving his way closer. He made another slow pass along the length of her, pausing briefly to dart his tongue inside. *Shit.* That felt better than anything he'd done yet, and she was torn between wanting him to linger and needing him to keep going.

One flick of his tongue against her clit, and her indecision vanished. Hell, she forgot how to breathe.

When he began circling back and forth, she shattered apart. But he wasn't finished. He eased off, just barely, before adding his lips to the mix, sucking at her while his tongue continued to play. She writhed in the tub, sloshing water everywhere.

As if that wasn't enough, Adrian slid two fingers inside her. She dimly worried that the webbing between them would impede his progress, but she needn't have. It was clearly flexible enough, and the feel of its lightly veined texture against her already sensitive skin added yet another layer to her bliss. His fingers worked her as his mouth continued his ministrations, and she nearly expired.

Opal grabbed the edge of the tub, her other hand still tangled in his hair, as her climax rocketed through her. It was a good thing she didn't have nearby neighbors; her shout could've drowned out the crashing of the ocean.

Adrian let her come down gently.

"Damn, Adrian," she whispered hoarsely. "That was…"

But the words died on her tongue. Because he *still* wasn't finished, apparently determined to show off just how long he could remain underwater.

When he finally lifted her utterly boneless form from the water, she'd lost count of her orgasms. Surely more than she'd thought humanly possible.

Not that she minded.

He sat her on the edge of the bath and placed a soft kiss on her forehead, while she could barely keep her blissfully dazed eyes open. When he finished gently drying her off, she vaguely registered his gentlemanly tossing of the towel on the floor to soak up the puddles, before he scooped her up once more. She nestled into the cradle of his arms with a contented hum.

"Gills are a wonderful invention," she mumbled against his chest.

The soft buzz of his chuckle against her cheek nudged her the last step of the way to dreamland, and she was asleep before they even reached the bed.

Chapter Fourteen

*M*onday dawned bright and clear—and with it, the realization of how much they'd let themselves get distracted when it came to planning for Adrian's work situation. What with all of their sharing and pleasuring, they had conveniently forgotten that, while he could get away with being "in costume" all day on set, he needed to get to the studio first.

Which was how he found himself in Opal's bedroom, staring at his shirt and pants without a clue how he was going to disguise himself on the trip to his dressing room.

"Any luck?" Opal came to stand next to him.

"Hmm?"

She nodded at the clothing. "You looked like you were willing them to grow big enough to fit over your new and improved body. Did it work?"

Adrian snorted. "Sadly, no." He fingered his necklace. "If only I could will this thing to turn me back. I'd settle for at least the car ride."

"It really did seem to glow a little brighter when you tried Saturday afternoon. Maybe you just need some more practice. That magic could be in you yet." She offered him an encouraging smile.

"Thanks for the vote of confidence, darling. But I think we'll need to make do for today."

"Oh! That reminds me. I found this." She pulled a large tan garment from behind her back.

"Is that…a trench coat?"

"It is. When I moved in here, my dad was worried about me getting caught in some colossal sea gale. I tried to point out that the southern California coast isn't exactly prone to those, but he insisted that I keep this, just in case." She shook her head with a fond smile. "It's his old one, and given the fact that he's very tall and I am…very not, I'm more likely to drown in this than in any actual rainfall. But that also means it should cover you nicely," she finished cheerfully.

"Huh." Adrian took the coat and held it up. It did look pretty roomy. "This might work. Thanks, Opal's dad." His smile dimmed, and he gestured to his head. "But what about all this? You can hardly drive down Hollywood Boulevard with this face in the passenger seat. Even the guards at the lot are going to think it's weird that I'm already in full makeup."

"I thought of that, too." Opal bit her lip, glancing warily at him. "I know it's not ideal, but I can throw a blanket in the car. Maybe you can scrunch down till we get there, and then cover up till we go through the gates?"

"Like I'm smuggled goods?"

She gave a little shrug. "You are worth quite a lot."

His chuckle settled into a sigh. "I suppose it'll have to do. Thank you, Opal."

In the end, he was a bit too tall to comfortably stuff himself far enough down in the front seat to evade notice. So, Adrian wound up lying across the back seat, both of them giggling most of the way to work.

Opal's usual parking spot near the makeup building was rather public, so she parked farther away, in a more isolated area, to avoid attention.

Naturally, his costar Yvette bounded up to the car before Opal had even turned off the engine.

"Hey, doll. You're here early. And since when do you park all the way over here?" Her voice sounded slightly muffled to Adrian, who remained huddled under the cover of his blanket.

"Oh. Sometimes I like to mix it up. Stretch my legs a little." Opal's voice sounded remarkably smooth and calm, considering their charade.

"I was just running to the commissary for some coffee. Want to join me?"

"You know, I'd love to, but...I have some stuff I've been putting off that I need to...catch up on before it's time to be on set. That's why I'm so early today."

"Gotcha. If you change your mind, you know where to find me!"

"Thanks. See you later, Yvette."

Adrian held his breath, waiting until Yvette's footsteps faded to peek out from under a corner of the blanket. After another moment, the car door next to his feet opened.

"Okay, the coast is clear," Opal whispered.

He threw the blanket off and blinked up at her. "She has impeccable timing."

"Tell me about it." She threw a glance all around and then beckoned with her hand. "Come on, you should be good."

Adrian sat up and eased out of the car, careful to crouch low just in case. Opal grabbed her bags, and then they were off, as quick as they could manage. They made their way between two soundstages, thankfully quiet at this hour, and Opal peered around the corner before they emerged. Just as quickly, she whipped back against the wall like a noir dame.

He couldn't help his smile. "You know, it's okay for *you* to be seen, Opal. You're not the sea creature."

"Ha-ha. I know. But Marge from wardrobe is over there, and the last thing we need is to come up with an explanation for your current sartorial splendor. She'll have it all over the lot, and twisted into something salacious, in five minutes."

"Fair enough."

They waited until it was safe, and then continued on their way. It took them nearly twenty minutes to get across the studio to Adrian's dressing room, as they dashed between buildings, dodging coworkers and potential gossips at every turn, Opal providing cover for him when necessary. He somehow managed to avoid detection, and they finally arrived at their destination.

Adrian shut the door behind them and slumped against it, exhausted in every sense of the word.

"Oh, that was much harder than I thought it would be," he wheezed.

"As the girl said to the soldier."

Adrian snorted, and then they both burst into laughter. He crossed the small room and pulled her in for a hug. They leaned on each other for a lovely, lingering moment. Then he sighed and let her go.

"So, we made it this far. What now, captain?"

"Right." Opal squared her shoulders. "Now, the real work begins. And then it should get pretty easy." She glanced around the room. "Let's ditch that coat and see just how accurately I captured you."

He dutifully stripped out of the trench and stood before her. She was all business now, assessing him from head to webbed toe.

"Should I scrap the sarong, too?" He'd left it on, just in case the coat parted while he walked. If he had been stopped along the way, that part of him certainly didn't match his suit.

"Not yet. We are gonna need to make sure that loincloth provides sufficient coverage, but we should start at the top. That might be where I need to do the most work." She reached for his mask, where it sat on a mannequin head on his dressing table. "Here, have a seat."

He did as he was told, watching as she flipped on the bright lights framing the mirror, then held up the head next to his own.

He sucked in a fascinated breath but held his tongue while her eyes flicked back and forth, taking in every detail in the mirror. When her fierce concentration started to ease, he felt safe in interrupting her examination.

"Opal."

"Hmm?"

"It's uncanny."

She blinked, her eyes finding his in the glass, and her face broke into a bright smile. "It really is, isn't it?"

He nodded, gesturing at his double reflection. "I mean, just look at me. I'm beside myself."

Opal groan-laughed and nudged his shoulder. "Enough with the corny. Let me get back to work."

He mimed locking his lips with a key, delighting in watching her genius in action.

She turned her attention to the back of his head—heads—and continued the inspection. She ran her fingers through his hair and shook her own head.

"God, I even got the length of your mane right," she murmured, almost to herself. Snapping out of her reverie, she continued with more volume. "Okay, I think we're good, actually. You can stand up. Let's make sure your back and fins match."

They continued their visual checkup for a few more minutes, both of them pausing now and then to marvel at the complete *lack* of work Opal had before her to maintain continuity between her creation and his own body.

Adrian finally swapped the bright sarong for his loincloth, and the non-transformation was complete.

Almost.

"Oh, shit," Opal muttered. "Your tattoo. I forgot all about it."

"Me too. I'm sorry."

She flashed him a smile. "No need to apologize. The only thing I don't like about it is the fact that I didn't think of it." She bit her lip, running her fingers over his arm with a hum. "I wonder…"

She turned to root through her makeup bag, and came back to

him with the light purple putty she often used to cover the seam between his mask and his suit if it didn't cooperate. She began applying it over his tattoo, first with her fingers, then a spongy tool. Her frown increased the more she worked.

"Damn."

"Everything okay?"

"No. This stuff is designed for human skin and works surprisingly well on rubber too." She grimaced. "But it doesn't seem to want to play well with yours. It covers some, but I'm not sure I like it. And I'm definitely worried about what'll happen when you get wet."

She stared critically at his arm, and he wished he could offer her some help. But she was the expert, and if she didn't know…

Opal drew in a sudden, sharp breath. "Huh. Maybe…" She fished through her bag again, coming up with a scrap of the material she'd used for his mask and a small bottle of brown liquid. "Mind if I try some spirit gum?"

He couldn't stop his now-straighter nose from wrinkling. "I do hate the stuff, but sure. If you think it'll work."

She smiled reassuringly while unscrewing the cap. "More often than not, this stuff isn't too nice on people's skin. Which is why it could cooperate on yours now." She paused, the little brush in her hand hovering above his arm. "But tell me if it stings or hurts or makes you feel weird in any way."

He nodded, and she bent to her task. Interestingly enough, the vile substance stung a hell of a lot less than it had whenever he'd donned fake mustaches and beards for his roles over the years he'd spent as a human.

Opal finished attaching the scrap to him and stepped back. "It might just work. I'll need a bigger piece to finish the job, but… Yeah." She raised triumphant eyes to his. "That's the ticket."

"Brilliant."

She checked her wristwatch. "Okay, we've still got plenty of time before you're called to set. I've got more of this stuff in my office, so I'll grab it and get back here to cover you up." Her gaze wandered down. "Speaking of cover... You think that'll be enough?"

"Funny, I was actually wondering the same thing. When you mentioned my being in the water, it got me thinking. This is fine if I'm standing still, but if I start moving...or this floats too much..."

"Those censors' heads will explode."

"And as much as I'd relish offending their delicate sensibilities, it's probably best not to rock the boat at this point."

"Right." She raised an eyebrow. "Want me to swing by the costume department and score you a dance belt? Might have to get a little creative to explain why you suddenly need one at this point, but I'll think of something."

Adrian chuckled. "I'm sure you would. But no need." He turned to search through a drawer in his closet, finding his quarry right away. "Aha." He held up a pair of swim trunks. "If I remember correctly, these were a little loose for my human thighs, so they should fit over my legs now."

"And they're skimpy enough to disappear under the loincloth. Nice."

They shared a grin.

"Okay," Opal continued, "I'll be back in a few. Are you good here?"

"I'm better than good." Relief coasted through him. "This is actually going to work, isn't it?"

"It is." She rose up on her toes to feather a kiss over his cheek. "Be right back."

Adrian watched the door snick closed behind her, inordinately grateful, after so many lonely years, to be part of a team. And a damn fine one at that.

FOR ALL INTENTS AND PURPOSES, his long day of filming went off with nary a hitch. Still, Adrian had grossly underestimated the mental toll of the stress of evading detection that loomed over him all day.

He'd technically been playing a role, keeping a secret, for the better part of a decade. But as long as he avoided love and relationships, the likelihood of his suddenly being revealed as not-quite-human was slim to none. Now that he was, in fact, a kelpie again, he spent the day in constant trepidation that someone would figure out he wasn't wearing a mask and a suit anymore—second-guessing every move, wanting to make sure he didn't have more, or less, ease of motion than he usually did.

Opal hovered nearby, surreptitiously checking the patch over his tattoo every chance she got. He avoided offers to take his "mask" off during the longer breaks between takes and hid in his dressing room during his lunch hour. Unfortunately, Opal had made lunch plans with a colleague from her department the week prior, so she couldn't join him. She offered to cancel, but he encouraged her not to—he wanted her to have a respite from their charade, even if he couldn't.

The hardest part of all, however, had nothing to do with his transformation. At countless moments throughout the day, he fought the overwhelming urge to show Opal his affection. He wanted to kiss her, take her hand, even just huddle next to her between takes. He caught her curbing her gravitation toward him more than a few times as well. But they'd agreed to keep their relationship quiet for the moment. As strong as their feelings were, it was still so new—and the last thing they needed was to incite studio gossip, on top of everything else.

So when the final take had been called and he was released to go home, Adrian slumped against his dressing room door once again, with every bit of the exhaustion and none of his earlier adrenaline rush.

And he wasn't finished yet.

He groaned. "Damn. I still have to get off this lot."

Opal turned to face him, all sympathy. "I think it might be easier this time."

"How do you figure?"

She smiled and pointed to a pile of clothing on his dresser that he hadn't noticed before. "I went to wardrobe on a foraging expedition during one of my breaks."

"You did?"

"I did. I also may have told them that I was there on your behalf, because you had a wild publicity idea to appear in places as your creature character, but in human clothes, and you wanted to try it out first before you took it to anyone higher up. They were very obliging, pulling up your measurements and grabbing me stuff that was a bit bigger. But you might have to follow through with the act at some point. Sorry."

Adrian chuckled. "That's...pretty great, actually. Thanks." He picked up the hat on top of the pile. "None of these will cover my face, though."

"No, but they'll do a much better job than just a trench coat. And we can use the publicity story if anyone stops you on the way to the car."

He set the hat on his head. It fit surprisingly well. But then he looked in the mirror. "I look ridiculous."

"Oh, come on. It's not that bad."

"Opal. People driving around Hollywood see a lot in their travels. But a fish in a fedora might be a bridge too far."

She gently turned him to face her. "First of all. You said it yourself: you're a mammal, not a fish."

He snickered at that.

"And—" She reached up to adjust the brim of his hat. "I think you look quite dapper."

"Well, you are the only one I'm truly interested in impressing, so I suppose there's that."

"See. I'm always right."

He groaned again and bent forward to lean his forehead against hers, under the hat. She kissed him softly.

"Come on. Get dressed and let's bounce."

"Deal."

Chapter Fifteen

*T*he next morning, Opal woke to a note on the pillow next to her.

Going for a swim. Be back soon. Love, A.

She smiled, hoping he'd find a little slice of peace in the water. Adrian had tried to put on a brave face when they returned to her place the night before, but she knew the day hadn't been easy on him.

She also anticipated the difficulties ahead for him, for them, once this picture wrapped in only a few more days. As much as it pained her to think about it, she wondered if he might need to return to his family for a little while—at the very least to get some answers to all his questions. But she had no idea if he'd be receptive to the suggestion. Or if she was ready to see him go.

Opal stretched and rose from the cozy cocoon of her bed. Though Adrian wasn't called to set and had a day off, she still had to go to work. She proceeded to get herself ready, but he had yet to return by the time she finished.

She glanced at the clock—still plenty of time before she needed to leave. She tossed her lipstick back in her bag and set off for the beach.

A folded towel sat on the rock in their little cove. Splashing sounds pulled her attention a little ways out to sea, where she spied her kelpie-man. But he wasn't alone. It looked like...

Opal's hand flew to her mouth. "Aww!"

An otter pup. Adrian was playing with an otter pup.

Talk about a splash...

She sank down onto the rock, content to watch the scene. After a few minutes, Adrian spotted her and waved cheerfully. He patted his small buddy on its furry head and started toward the shore. The pup made as if to follow him—she didn't blame the little cutie in the slightest—but stopped at the sound of a deep hum. For the first time, Opal noticed a full-sized otter hovering nearby, clearly a parent curbing its young's fun. She chuckled at the little whining sound the pup let out as it swam back in the opposite direction.

Adrian emerged, dripping and glistening, and loped across the sand to her. "Good morning."

"Morning. Made a friend, did you?"

He picked up the towel and began drying off. "I did. The little guy came right up to me. Mom didn't look too happy about it, and I worried she was going to charge, but she backed off when she realized I meant no harm."

"You are very friendly and approachable."

"Thank you, my dear." He wrapped the towel around his waist and bent down for a kiss. Then he sat down with a heavy sigh.

"You okay?"

He nodded. "Still processing, is all." He offered her a small smile. "Yesterday was a lot."

"At least you get a break today."

"Yeah. I'm sorry you don't."

Opal shrugged. "It's okay." She gave his knee a squeeze. "I've got a lot less to mull over than you do."

He huffed, eyes trained on the horizon. "As upset as I was when I first became human, I never let myself dwell on what I left behind, what would've been. Sure, I missed my home and the people I had to say goodbye to, but…I moved on. Made a brand-new life for myself. And as lonely as it's been, it's…"

"Yours."

"Mine." He met her gaze again. "Obviously, it's not what I planned when I was younger. But I…like who I've become. I like being an actor. I like the idea of taking you on real dates." He gestured at the water. "But then, that felt wonderful too. I'm torn in two, as if…"

"Everything and nothing is possible, all at once?" Opal asked softly.

A surprised whisper of laughter escaped him, the air from his gills coasting over her. "That's it exactly."

She sifted her fingers through his hair, still damp and salty from his swim. "You know, impossible as it sounds, all of it is who you are."

"I'm realizing that." He exhaled. "Gods, I wish I knew where I go from here."

"I wish I could help." She wove her arm through his and leaned her head on his shoulder. "It's too bad I can't seem to activate that magic honeypot of mine again and change you back and forth at will."

Adrian's shoulder vibrated with laughter under her cheek. "Maybe we should keep trying."

"Fine by me."

He planted a kiss on the crown of her head. By silent mutual agreement, they decided that any magical practice could wait till later, and they settled into a contented quiet, watching the waves lap at the shore.

Opal wanted to ease his burdens so very much. If only…

A dark shape surfaced briefly, farther out on the water. The otters were long gone, or so she'd thought. Opal continued to catch a few flashes of the shadowy form, but she couldn't be sure if she really saw something, or if the waves were playing tricks on her. But no. That was definitely a fin of some kind.

"Is that a dolphin?" she asked.

A larger silhouette started to emerge, and Adrian's entire body stiffened. She lifted her head to look at him.

"No. That's not a dolphin." His voice took on an unusual tone. "That's my mother."

"Your… What…?" Her attention snapped back to the ocean.

The figure had come much closer to shore, and Opal could see now that she looked very much like Adrian. Same gray-purple, iridescent skin, same pointed ears. Her facial features were a bit softer, and her body sported more curves. Her black hair was nearly waist-length and threaded with silver. But there was no doubt she and Adrian were related. She looked quite stunning.

He stood slowly, and Opal followed suit. Her heart pounded an erratic rhythm in her chest, and Adrian gripped her hand tightly, before freezing into an immobile statue beside her.

The sea-woman fully emerged, making her way slowly toward them through the waves. She wore a dress-like garment that seemed to be woven from strips of kelp in varying shades. Opal dimly noted that it was rather stylish, for something made of seaweed.

She stopped a few feet from them. "Hello, Adrian."

"Mother." He swallowed audibly, his melodic voice all gravel. "What are you doing here?"

Her gaze flickered briefly to Opal before darting back to her son. She reached up to tuck a wayward strand of hair behind her ear, and Opal noticed a slight tremble. *She's nervous.*

"A few days ago, my magic…shivered, and I…I sensed that things had…changed for you." She gestured vaguely at the ocean behind her. "And I saw you, here." She hesitated. "I know I have no right, but…I wanted to see if you were all right."

Her eyes blazed, the same vibrant violet as her son's, and Opal could see the wealth of feeling behind them. Knew she was telling the truth. At the same time, she felt the pulse of Adrian's hand flexing around hers. She squeezed back, offering him what comfort she could.

"I…um…" Adrian shook his head and glanced down at Opal.

"Sorry. Opal, this is my mother, Larissa. Mother, this is Opal, my…" He smiled sweetly down at her. "My Opal."

She gave him—and herself—a moment to bask in their love, before turning her attention to Larissa, who regarded her with an unreadable expression.

Opal didn't know the proper etiquette in a situation like this—meeting your new beau's mother for the first time, when she was some kind of kelpie sorceress who'd accidentally cursed him and probably wasn't too thrilled that he'd gone and fallen in love with a human woman. Were they supposed to shake hands? She wasn't sure she wanted to, given what Larissa had inflicted on her son. And besides, then she'd have to let go of Adrian's, and that hardly seemed worth it.

So Opal settled for inclining her head.

Larissa did the same. "Opal. It's lovely to meet you."

"I honestly don't know that it's likewise." The words tumbled out before she could stop them, and she bit her lip.

But Larissa didn't flinch. Instead, she gave a small nod. "That's more than fair, given the circumstances."

"Oh." This woman was certainly not what she'd expected. But then, despite the tempestuous relationship between his parents, the two of them *had* raised Adrian into the remarkable man he was, so they must have some redeeming qualities lurking somewhere.

A strained silence stretched between their little trio, until the loud cry of a seagull broke the spell.

Larissa spoke first, her question tentative. "Might we talk for a bit?"

Adrian sighed heavily. "I…I don't know." He glanced down at Opal, his nerves clear.

She caressed her thumb across the back of his hand. "You do have questions, love," she whispered.

His eyes drifted closed for a moment, and then he nodded.

"I should let you get to it."

Adrian's small tug on her arm felt almost panicked. "You don't have to go."

"You two have a lot to talk about, and I imagine it'll be easier for you without a third party, no? Besides, I have to get to work soon."

"Oh. Right." A thread of tension lingered in his voice.

She really did believe that they'd be freer to speak without her added presence, but she didn't want to abandon him if he needed the support. She reached up to cup his cheek. "But if you need me to stay, I can call in sick."

He smiled and covered her hand with his. "No, it's okay. I'll be fine." He kissed her palm. "Thanks."

"I'll see you tonight." At his nod, she squared her shoulders and faced his mother. "Larissa."

"Opal." Larissa's lips curved in a small smile of appreciation.

She wouldn't exactly say she trusted the sea-woman, but that tiny expression eased some of Opal's nerves about leaving. As she crested the dune leading to the cove, she shot one more glance over her shoulder, willing some of her strength into Adrian's heart.

Chapter Sixteen

*A*drian watched Opal go before turning back to his mother. An abundance of emotion roiled within him. He was stunned to see Larissa again, and part of him wanted to turn around and follow Opal, not talk to his mother at all. But Opal was right. He had questions that needed answering.

And as much as he hated to admit it, a not-so-small part of him simply wanted to hug her. Despite everything, she was his mom, after all.

He erred on the side of caution, raising his eyebrows, waiting for her to make the first move.

"How...how are you?" Larissa breathed. To her credit, her nerves didn't seem like an act.

"Okay, I guess. Considering."

"I know it might not mean much, and I'm not looking for any kind of forgiveness, but I truly am sorry, Adrian. For everything."

He nodded, unsure how else to respond.

"I have missed you, terribly."

He forced his voice out. "How did you know where to find me?"

"I've always kept an eye on you. Even got hold of a few

human newspapers from time to time. I wanted to make sure you were doing okay."

He couldn't contain his surprise. "So many times, I felt like someone was out there…"

She inclined her head. "It was me. Well, me or your father."

"So you haven't killed each other yet."

A sad smile crossed her lips. "No. As a matter of fact, we're… much better now. Patched things up after we both realized what utter fools we'd been. It's been…nice. Good."

He huffed, unable to hide his sarcasm. "I tried for years. And all it took was my being cursed and leaving you on your own. Who knew?"

"Losing you was hitting ocean bottom for both of us." She held up a staying hand. "And I know that's no excuse. But we finally realized what all our feuding had cost, for everyone around us—and each other. We'd been hurting you for quite some time, even before the curse, hadn't we?"

His throat felt hot and tight. "Yeah," he croaked.

Larissa reached out to touch him, but stopped herself. "If I could take it all back, I would. You have no idea how much I want to." She sniffed. "I realize our relationship is likely beyond repair, and you have no reason to trust me, but…" She straightened her spine and held his gaze. "I am here to help you. In any way I can."

Adrian believed her. It was too soon to know if they could have any kind of relationship, but he at least appreciated her offer.

Just that morning, he'd had a million questions. But they were all stuck, inaccessible now. Only one made it through the chaos inside him. An important one.

"Can I ever…be human again?" He trained his eyes on the horizon, afraid to look at her.

She took a moment in answering, and Adrian held his breath.

"I can't say for certain, but it might be possible." He finally met her eye, her expression serious, almost wary. "If you wanted to. Would you…want to?"

"Yes." The force of his answer surprised him, but doubts

followed immediately. "Maybe. I think." He shook his head, pacing away from her, his words tumbling out fast. "It's all I've been able to think about for days. I was *just* telling Opal...I feel so split. This is me. But I've been human for a while now, and I like that, too. And it sure as hell would make things easier, in a lot of ways."

Larissa's voice was soft, and closer behind him than he expected. "She seems lovely. And feisty."

He turned to face his mother. "She's magnificent."

Larissa smiled. "I would expect nothing less for my boy." Catching herself, she glanced away for a moment. "And I can see how much she cares for you. How much you care for each other."

Adrian nodded.

"Do you remember Helena, the elder who came to visit from time to time when you were small?"

"Sure. We used to drive her crazy, asking her to do magic tricks for us. She's the sorceress who trained you, isn't she?"

"She is." She inhaled deeply. "I reached out to her right after everything that happened with you and the necklace. It took a lot of finagling to get her to talk to me when she found out what I'd done with my magic, but...she finally did. We've chatted a lot since." She raised intense eyes to his. "I wanted to be prepared for every scenario, ready to help you through, if you'd let me. And I knew there was a high likelihood that you'd fall in love with a human." She lowered her head again. "I'll be honest, I thought it might happen sooner."

He swallowed against the memory of how solitary he'd kept himself before meeting Opal. "I wasn't in much of a rush."

"It must have been awfully lonely for you," she whispered.

He managed a nod.

She shook herself, taking them back to business. "Anyway, Helena has a lot of wisdom to offer. I can take you to her—"

Adrian jerked to attention. "Wait. You said *you* could help me."

"I can. Through Helena."

He took a step back. "I can't just pick up and leave." The thought of being away from Opal especially pained him.

"But you can't exactly stay here like this, can you?"

He crossed his arms, his anger returning. "And whose fault is that?"

Larissa sighed. "Mine. I *know* that. But Helena doesn't travel anymore. And she knows far more than I do."

Adrian rubbed the back of his neck, closing his eyes. Anger wasn't helping. But if this woman might, he owed it to himself, and to Opal, to seek her out.

He opened his eyes on a sigh. "If you think Helena is my best chance, then I'll go. But I need to get through this week first. I have obligations at the studio."

Relief and confusion warred on his mother's face, before the questions won out. "Obligations? *Human* obligations?"

He tightened the reins on his frustration. Barely. "Yes, Mother. I have a job. Commitments."

"To your...moving pictures?" She was clearly trying to understand, but her lip curled ever so slightly on the words, and his patience nearly snapped.

"Those moving pictures saved me," he gritted out. "Did you know that? When I was first on my own, every day I set aside money from my job to go to the pictures. Every day, tired or not, I sat in the back of that dark theater, watching. Learning how to be human." His lips curved upward at the memory. "And when I saw the ad for stunt performers out in California—who could *swim*—I couldn't believe my luck."

He raised his eyes to hers, willing her to understand. "It was better than I could've imagined. As my roles got bigger, better, I found out I *like* acting. Putting on someone else's shoes. And yeah, it was lonely. But I carved out this life for myself, and it's *mine*. And it led me to Opal. I wouldn't trade her for the world."

Larissa stared at him for a long moment, and he could see understanding in her eyes now. Along with something suspiciously resembling pride.

"All right, then." She nodded. "I can probably change you back long enough to get you through a few days."

He blinked a few times, unsure if he'd heard her correctly. "You…you can? But you said…"

"Now that the curse is broken, my magic will only be powerful enough to change you for the short-term, if that. That's why we need Helena. It's a bit of a long story, but she has a few theories. Which she can't confirm until she sees you herself." She took a step closer, venturing to lay a gentle hand on his arm. "But if it's what you want, I'll do my best to get you the time you need until then."

Adrian's head spun. It was all so much. Despite his well-founded reservations, he wanted to trust his mother. At least in this. She and Helena were his best, his *only*, way to find the solutions he sought. And he needed to try. For Opal. For himself. For their future.

He nodded. "Okay. Let's do it."

Chapter Seventeen

*O*pal returned home that evening with cautious optimism. She parked her car and scanned the beach in front of her, but there was no sign of Adrian or his mother. She had no idea if Larissa had any inclination to stick around, or if her son would even welcome that. But she hoped the day had at least brought Adrian some small solace.

For one fleeting moment, she worried he might not be there when she opened her door, that his mother had spirited him away through the waves. Then she immediately chided herself. Despite her imagination's uncanny accuracy of late, this was no time to let it run away with her.

Still, she held her breath as she fit her key into the lock.

His warm, soothing voice met her the minute she stepped over the threshold. "Hello, Opal."

"Hi— Oh." She blinked for a moment, watching Adrian rise from the couch.

Human Adrian.

"Wow. You're…"

He glanced down at himself, almost sheepishly. "Yeah. For now."

Opal set her bags down by the door, mind reeling. She was

relieved to see him, relieved he had an easier way to get through their last few days of filming. But at the same time, disappointment wove through her. She rather liked him in his kelpie form too.

Curiosity pushed its way to the forefront of her mind. "What, um…what does 'for now' mean, exactly?"

"Apparently, our breaking the curse portends that my mother's magic can't hold for too long." He shook his head. "I'm still trying to work it all out myself. But she bought me a few days to finish the picture. We hope." He flashed her a crooked smile. "I'm going to need your help, watching out for purple spots or sudden fin reappearances."

"That, I can manage." She hesitated. "And after we finish the week?"

"Right." He took her hand. "I…I'm going to have to go away for a little bit."

It was nothing she hadn't expected, been ready to suggest it even, but it still pained her.

"Come here." Adrian led her to the couch. "There's an elder among our kind, Helena, who knows all the ins and outs of kelpie magic. My mother believes she can help. They've been consulting about me for years, I guess. But in order to come to any conclusions, Helena needs to actually meet me."

"And would you change back into this form permanently, then? Is that what you want?"

He sighed. "Honestly, the more I think about it, the more sure I am that…in a perfect world…I'd love to change back and forth at will, just like we joked. Does that sound crazy?"

Opal couldn't contain her grin. "Are you kidding? That sounds wonderful. I meant what I said this morning. You're *you* in both forms." She bit her lip. "And I have to admit, as much as I love this version, I was a little disappointed not to see you as a kelpie when I got here tonight."

His smile took on a cheeky edge. "I see how it is. You just want me for my underwater skills."

"What can I say? A gal really hasn't had her canyon properly yodeled in until it happens underwater and"—she shivered at the glorious memory—"*that* enduringly."

Adrian brought her hand up to his lips with a laugh. "Rest assured, my dear Opal, I am more than happy to yodel in your canyon anytime, anywhere. In any form."

Another shiver rocketed through her. "Okay, that's enough of that. I have more questions before we start ravishing each other again."

He chuckled. "Fair enough. Rain check."

She nodded. "Good. So…is it possible? Can this Helena person actually make it happen?"

"Could be. Or…" His cheeks flushed. "I can."

"You?"

"Mm-hmm." He rubbed the back of his neck. "She suspects I might have some latent talents in that arena after all."

"See, I told you."

"I had never bothered to learn much about the nuances of it all, but apparently, what can make it finally kick in is…a trigger of sorts."

"Like, say, a curse?"

"Yeah." He huffed. "There's still a good chance I don't have the ability, though."

"But Helena will be able to tell. Which is why you need to go to her."

Adrian nodded. "I do. If there's any possibility…"

She squeezed his hand. "Of course. I understand. You know, before your mother showed up this morning, I thought of suggesting a visit to your family."

"You did?"

"Sure. You need answers. And you're clearly not going to get them here."

He smiled softly, gratefully.

"So where exactly does Helena live?" Opal asked. "You mentioned once that you grew up in the Atlantic?"

"I did. Not far from the New England coastline." He heaved a sigh. "But Helena lives in the waters off Scotland."

"Oh. That's…a bit farther than I was expecting."

Adrian took both her hands in his and shifted to face her more fully. "I wish you could come with me…"

"I'd hardly survive the depths of the ocean, would I?"

"No. But I promise, I will return to you as soon as I possibly can."

"I know."

Their eyes held for a long moment, filled with all their unspoken promises. Adrian rested his forehead against hers.

"I love you, Opal."

"And I love you, Adrian."

THEY MADE it through the remaining days of *The Kelp-Dweller from Fathoms Below*, filling their nights with as much of each other as they could until sleep came for them. Before they knew it, the picture had wrapped. And Larissa's magic, which had held up remarkably well, even with all of their nighttime activity, finally started to wear off.

Saturday dawned, bright and clear, and Opal stood with Adrian, fully back in kelpie form, in their little cove. Larissa hovered a distance away in the waves, giving them privacy for their farewell. He'd arranged for time off from the studio, claiming a family emergency, and was about to set off.

Neither of them felt quite ready for his journey.

"I wish I could guarantee this will work," Adrian breathed.

"Even if it doesn't, we'll figure something out." She framed his face with her hands. "We'll find a way."

He nodded, cupping her own face in return. "Together."

Their mouths came together, lingering, exploring. Savoring. Opal tasted salt, despite the fact that neither of them had been in the water. She wasn't sure whose tears they were—or if Adrian was capable of crying in this form, come to think of it.

They finally broke apart, resting their foreheads together.

"I'm going to miss you so fucking much," she whispered.

"Right back at you."

She pulled back to look into his vibrant violet eyes. "Come back to me."

"Always."

He stepped back and glanced down at the sand, a smile spreading across his face. He bent to pick something up, holding out his hand to her. A small starfish rested in his palm.

"Make a wish."

Opal chuckled. "A wish?"

"Sure." He lifted one shoulder. "You can't always see the stars from the depths of the ocean, so we kelpies make do with these, too."

She gave this lovely, wonderful man a watery smile and rested her palm over his, sandwiching the starfish between them. They locked eyes as they made presumably the same wish. Too soon, he flipped his hand over, leaving the tiny creature behind as he slid out of her grasp.

One last, lingering kiss. And then he waded reluctantly into the lapping waves. A bit farther out, he turned to blow her a kiss. She mimed catching it and clutching it to her heart, and the flash of his smile reached her across the distance.

Opal kept that kiss pressed to her heart, watching the horizon long after Adrian melted into it.

SHE MANAGED BETTER than she expected at work, despite the constant reminders of him everywhere she turned. Though she was relieved, at least, not to have another monster film on the docket, more than ready to throw herself into simple human makeup for the time being.

Near the end of the third week of his absence, all hell broke loose at Neptune Pictures.

Opal had an atypically late call time, so she didn't arrive at the studio until midday, only to find an unusual buzz in the air. She couldn't quite put her finger on it, but something was off. A frantic, frenetic energy bounced off everyone she saw.

Yvette ambushed her at the door to the makeup building.

"Where have you been?"

Opal smirked. "Good day to you, too. I had the morning off. What gives?"

Yvette ignored her ribbing and gripped her arm as they entered the building. "You would not believe what has been going on around here." At Opal's blank look, she gave an exasperated huff. "Didn't you see the papers?"

"No. I was...busy." No need to admit she'd given in to her desire to sit on the beach for a few hours, staring hopefully—or maybe hopelessly—out to sea.

"Arthur Ronson's *out* as head of the studio."

That snapped Opal out of her moony thoughts, and she almost tripped on the carpet. "No shit."

"Yup." Her friend's eyes brightened. "And you will never guess who's in charge now." She barely paused before answering herself. "Lois Ashford."

Opal blinked, unsure she'd heard correctly. "That diva actress? Wait, didn't she start out here at Neptune? There must be one hell of a juicy story there."

"Oh, you know it."

"So, what do you think the odds are she's not nearly the royal bitch the papers make her out to be?"

They smirked ruefully before answering together, "Pretty high."

Opal groaned, pausing as they neared her office. "I don't even want to know what I'm walking into right now—Mort being one of Arthur's cronies and all."

"Good luck, hon."

Yvette fled in search of more gossip, while Opal braced herself to deal with her boss.

What she didn't expect was to find him in *her* office...rooting through one of her file drawers.

She stopped in the doorway, crossing her arms in an effort to keep a lid on her anger. She wished Adrian was nearby with his water tank. Preston's head popped up when he saw her.

"Oh, good. You're here. You picked a fine day to sleep in."

She wanted to retort that he'd given her the morning off, but refrained. There was a strong chance flames might shoot out of her mouth if she did, and she'd hate for any of her sketches to get singed.

He continued anyway. "It's unbelievable. Ronson's been kicked out. Of his own studio!"

"I heard," she gritted out.

"It's chaos around here. Who knows what torture that harpy's about to inflict. But no need to worry." Opal wasn't, but she didn't bother to say so. "I've got us covered. Lots of leads already. And I want to be prepared. Do you have those sketches from the outer space picture last year?"

So that explained his rummaging.

"They're not in there." She sure as hell wasn't about to tell him where they actually were. Although she wouldn't mind telling him where he could shove them...

One of his words caught up to her.

"I'm sorry, did you say *us*?"

He turned to face her with a stupidly smug smile. "I sure did, little lady. Don't fret. You don't think I'd jump ship without my gal Friday, do you?" He winked. Actually *winked*. "Find me those drawings, would you? I want to include them in the portfolio."

Opal gaped as he brushed past her. *Gal Friday, my ass.* She had no idea what her future held with this new studio boss, but if

Mort Preston thought she'd go anywhere with him, he could keep dreaming.

She'd barely set her things down and shut the drawer he'd so rudely left open when a hush fell outside her office door. She poked her head out to see none other than Lois Ashford herself strolling in—coolly sophisticated, gorgeous, not a trace of "harpy" about her.

Opal hovered in her doorway, watching as Preston strode out of his own office. He planted himself in what he no doubt assumed was a blatant power posture, feet wide and arms crossed, rather petulantly, over his chest. Establishing dominance, or some such bullshit.

Lois stopped in front of him with a pleasant smile. "Mr. Preston. I wanted to stop by and formally introduce myself. I'm looking forward to working with you."

Her tone dripped with sweetness, but Opal detected a lack of sincerity behind it. She liked the woman already.

"I'll be honest, Ms. Ashford," the toad responded, "I'm not entirely sure we will be working together."

"Oh? That's a shame. Your department does some wonderful work."

Her calm, collected demeanor—along with the compliment he didn't deserve—seemed to rattle him. "Well... I... That is..." He cleared his throat roughly, absently gesturing in Opal's direction. "I'll have you know we've already received several offers. From studios where I know we'll be appreciated."

"We?" The word came out before Opal could keep the venom from her tone.

Lois's observant gaze flicked briefly to her, while Preston ignored her completely.

He continued, "You know, Arthur Ronson valued this department's contributions greatly, especially our monsters. How can I be assured we'll be permitted to carry on, now that he's been ousted, hmm? I've seen how this goes. 'Twas beauty killed the beast, after all." His amusement at what he considered his witty joke warred with his pathetically haughty air.

Opal snorted. "Please. Beauty didn't kill the beast, patriarchy did," she muttered.

"Excuse me?" Preston's utter confusion might have been funny under other circumstances.

Opal wasn't sure why she kept going, but her mouth seemed to have developed a mind of its own. "It was patriarchy. Beauty and beast were becoming friends, and it wouldn't be long before everyone realized that the beast was not, in fact, the monstrous party in this scenario. So patriarchy took down the beast, in so-called defense of beauty's honor, thus pinning guilt and blame on beauty's shoulders, and ensuring everyone stays in their rightful place."

The thought of anything like that happening to Adrian pierced her heart with a shard of ice, and she finished with a sneer.

Only to find all eyes pinned on her. Silent and relatively stunned.

Shit.

"Right. But that's neither here nor there, is it?" She attempted a weak laugh. "You two clearly have a lot to discuss, so I'm just going to...get back to work. Ms. Ashford, it was lovely to meet you. Welcome."

Opal turned and made a beeline for her office. She closed the door behind her and sank against it. This day was turning out just great. Her boss was trying to poach her away to another studio, on top of taking his usual credit for her work. She'd just run her mouth off and made a fool of herself in front of her new big boss. She prayed she'd still have a job *anywhere* tomorrow.

And she couldn't even share any of it with Adrian.

Chapter Eighteen

*I*n an entirely predictable turn of events, when Opal arrived at her office the next morning, Mort Preston was nowhere to be found. His office door closed, the lights off. She was tempted to peek in and see if he'd already removed his things, but kept her curiosity in check.

To her great relief, there was also an absence of pink slips on her desk.

The mood around the department was quiet, everyone keeping their heads down, despite the hum of nervous—and curious—energy zinging amongst them. She'd kill to be able to trade gossip and opinions with Adrian. But she had no idea when he'd be back.

Opal sat down, prepared to focus on her work through sheer force of will. A knock at her door interrupted her progress before she even started.

"Good morning, Ms. Prince," a cheerful studio page greeted her. "Message for you."

She accepted his proffered slip of paper with a murmur of thanks, and he was gone in a flash. Opal opened the note, and her stomach sank. It was an invitation of sorts.

To Lois Ashford's office.

The studio head had left the meeting's timing open-ended, requesting that Opal drop by "at her convenience." She gulped as she stood. Better get it over with; no point in delaying the inevitable.

Opal made her way as quickly as she could. The mood all over the lot was much the same as within her department—the buzz much quieter than the previous day, but present nonetheless.

When she arrived at her destination, her new boss greeted her warmly, inviting her to take a seat across from her at the desk. Opal glanced around the room briefly, noting that the place somehow appeared classier already.

"I apologize for the formal summons," Lois began, "but I figured it might be easier for us to talk here"—she raised a perfectly sculpted eyebrow—"and give your peers less fodder for gossip."

Opal chuckled nervously. "That's a fair assessment."

"Let's get right down to it, shall we? As you might have guessed, Mort Preston stepped down this morning. And he sent a most...interesting resignation letter." Lois handed a sheet of paper across the desk to Opal.

She took it and started skimming.

"That *bastard*." The roach actually had the nerve to include Opal in this garbage. She snapped her head up. "You should know, I did not sign off on this."

Lois's lips curved upward. "I suspected as much. Preston seems to have failed to realize his contract did not include you. Or even his department's designs. Those belong to the studio." She smiled at Opal's surprise. "I realize this is a big change for everyone here, and you're under no obligation to stay, of course. But I do hope, in spite of your former boss's misguided notions, that you decide to remain. I would like to work with you."

"Thank you."

Lois rested her elbows on the desk, clasping her hands. "You know, I have another suspicion—that most of Neptune's best makeup designs have been yours, not his."

Opal's breath caught in her chest. Out of old, sadly necessary habits, she thought of prevaricating for one brief second. But this was a new day, and she no longer worked for Mort Preston or Arthur Ronson. A flash of memory—Preston sputtering and drenched, Adrian's satisfied smirk—gave her the boost she needed. Time to be bold.

She squared her shoulders, looked Lois directly in the eye, and spoke clearly. "They have been. He took credit for most of them, but the designs were mine. Including what I consider my proudest work to date, the sea creature we just wrapped. *The Kelp-Dweller from Fathoms Below.*"

"All right, then."

She saw nothing but respect in Lois's gaze, and her spirits lifted.

"If you don't mind my asking, what's going to happen with that one? Will it still be released?" Opal didn't know if this was the right time to bring it up, but she wanted the world to see not only her work, but Adrian's. Especially considering it could be his last picture.

Can't think about that now.

"Don't worry, it is still going forward. Roger and several of the producers appear willing to stay on here, and the legal team assures me that all our completed and near-completed projects can see the light of day. I want to make sure everyone's hard work is rewarded."

"That's good. Thank you."

"Speaking of hard work and rewards... That brings me to the primary reason I invited you here today." Lois paused. "I'd like you to take over Mr. Preston's position, as the new head of makeup here at the studio."

Opal's jaw nearly hit the floor. "Me?"

"Of course. You've clearly been the brains behind the operation for quite some time. Your talent is tremendous, and from what I've already been able to gather, you've garnered the respect of a great many of your colleagues. You're the natural choice."

"Wow."

I'm going to wake up from this dream any minute now, aren't I?

"Are you interested in the promotion?" Lois asked.

"I…" Opal blinked, heart pounding in her chest. "Yes."

Lois smiled. "Good. I like your confidence." She held up her hand. "I do know what a big change this will be, though. So why don't you take a little time? Think through details and logistics, any possible concerns you might have. Then we'll come up with a plan to make this work for you and the department. Exactly the way you want it."

It was a heady offer. "I can do that."

"Excellent. Thanks for coming by today."

"Thank *you*." She stood along with Lois. "And good luck. You've got quite the battle ahead, I fear."

"Don't I know it."

They shared a smile. As Opal neared the door, she couldn't help voicing one last question before she left.

"If Preston hadn't quit, would this have still been your plan?"

"It would. I intended to fire him, but he saved me the trouble. And you've been overlooked for far too long." Lois's smile turned sly. "Though to be perfectly honest, *'twas patriarchy killed the beast* is what truly sealed your fate."

Opal laughed heartily.

She was going to like working for this woman.

SHE CALLED out to Adrian as soon as she walked through her front door that night. And promptly deflated when reality caught up to her.

She so desperately wanted to share her news with him.

She dropped her bags with a heavy sigh, then immediately turned and headed back out. If she couldn't be with him, she could watch the horizon and pretend he was on his way back. His little otter friend might even swim by to cheer her up. At the very least, the sunset would be pretty.

Her thoughts churned as she made her way across the beach. She wanted nothing more than to celebrate, but it felt empty without Adrian. It was agony not being able to reach out to him in any way.

Opal settled on their cozy rock seat, attempting to quiet her mind. The sinking sun was already painting its vibrancy across the waves, so it was a moment before she realized the dark shape taking form on the horizon was indeed a shape, and not the restless tide.

She held her breath, afraid to blink.

Could it be?

Before long, a head popped up over the surface of the water. An iridescent, violet head, with a long, dark mane of hair and eyes that shone bright even from a distance. Opal shot to her feet.

He swam closer, emerging little by little. He wore what looked like a pair of shorts, fashioned out of the same stylishly woven kelp as his mother's dress, and a bag slung over his shoulder. When he was almost fully out of the water, he held up his arms invitingly.

Opal closed the distance between them, sloshing through the surf and flinging herself at Adrian.

He nearly fell backward but held his ground, his arms circling around her and holding tight.

"God, I'm glad to see you," she whispered into his neck.

"Me too."

They clung to each other, the lapping waves tickling at their legs. It wasn't long before Opal desperately needed to see his face. She pulled back to frame him with her hands.

"You're here."

His cheeks lifted into a smile under her hands. "Did you doubt me?"

She let out a watery laugh. "Of course not. But you have no idea how much I wanted—needed—to see you today."

"Fateful timing as always, then."

"It is." She shook her head, truly taking him in for the first time, her news content to simmer while she drank him in. "How are you? What happened? You're still...you. Not that that's a bad thing," she finished in a rush.

"No, it's not. But as a matter of fact, I have the very best tidings." His grin widened. "Helena was right. As were you. I do have magic in me. It's technically not too powerful on its own, but..." He slipped his hand between them to grasp his necklace. "She taught me how to re-enchant it. So I can change back and forth. At will."

"Just like we hoped," she breathed.

"Yeah." He chuckled ruefully. "I'd show you now, but it's going to take me some more practice before I can do it quickly, without much concentration. And I'd much rather focus on holding you right now."

She tightened her arms around his neck. "Good plan."

Unable to resist any longer, they both leaned in for a kiss. Their moans mingled as they sank into each other, tongues reacquainting deliciously. When they finally broke for air, they rested their foreheads against each other, both panting.

A snatch of their earlier conversation caught up to Opal. "You said your magic wasn't strong on its own. Did Helena have to add hers to the mix? Or your mom?"

"No. Apparently this magic gets an extra boost from emotion. The same emotion that unlocked the curse in the first place." He smiled down at her. "Our love can, indeed, work wonders."

Said love blazed into a wildfire in her chest. "Can it, now?"

He nodded. "So we can start creating that life we want. I can visit my family and also go back to work at Neptune."

Mention of the studio brought her day roaring back.

"About that... I have some phenomenal news of my own! You would not believe what's been going on around here."

"Oh?"

Opal led him to their rock and dished out all the dirt. After her grand finale, he stared for a moment, shock written all over his face.

He opened his mouth several times before words made it out. "I don't even know where to begin." He flashed that lovely, crooked smile of his, face beaming. "Actually, that's not true. Opal, congratulations! You deserve this, my love. I'm so happy for you."

Tears sprang to her eyes. "Thanks." She chuckled. "Who knew we'd end up here when you pushed Preston in that pool?"

He laughed. "I must say, that was one of my proudest moments." He trailed a finger down her cheek. "Was that really only a few weeks ago? I feel like we've lived several lifetimes since."

"We sure have." She bit her lip as she looked up at him, her breath catching in her throat. "So this is what it feels like to have everything I could possibly want."

"Pretty spectacular, isn't it."

She nodded, and they shared another languid kiss. He broke off this time, with a startled noise deep in his throat.

"Speaking of everything, I almost forgot. I have something for you." He reached into his bag, pulling out a necklace similar to his own. "Here."

Opal took it gingerly. "It's beautiful. Just like yours."

"Exactly like mine."

At his pointed tone, she looked up. "Exactly?"

"Mm-hmm." His expression was wary, nervous. "I know we never talked about it, but I wanted you to have the option. If you'd like."

Opal stared. "The option. To change into…"

"Yes. If you want to." His words rushed out. "There's no pressure, of course. But I'd love to introduce you to my family. Show you where I grew up. This would make it possible."

All her excitement vanished as panic gripped her, her breath shallowing. The sentiment was lovely. But she realized with a jolt that there was something quite crucial that she'd never told Adrian. Something that was about to bite her firmly in the ass.

She swallowed hard. "Adrian, I…" She placed the necklace back in his hand, closing his fingers around it. "I can't. I'm sorry."

"Oh." He tried to hide it, but his face fell. "Right. You can't see yourself…" He trailed off, gesturing at his body.

"No! That's not it. I would love to try, really I would. But I… can't."

"I understand."

"No, you don't." She pushed to her feet with a whimper. She *really* should have come clean about this sooner. "I don't know why I didn't tell you. I should have. It's ironic, really." She hung her head. "So ironic."

"Opal, what is it?"

She turned back to face him, taking in his concerned expression.

"Ohhhh, I don't want to admit this."

Adrian stood and took her hands in his. "Opal, you can tell me anything."

She glanced out to sea, unable to meet his eyes, and mumbled her confession.

"I'm sorry, what?" She couldn't tell if he hadn't heard her, or if comprehension was the problem.

She gulped, forcing her voice louder.

"I can't swim."

He stared. "That's what I thought you said."

She pulled out of his grip and paced away from him. "I know; it's wild. But I just never learned as a kid. And then I tried when I was older and it…didn't go too well. I can barely even float." She threw her hands up in defeat. "And then I go and fall for a fucking sea god! How unbelievable is that! And you expect me to transform my hopeless self into this magnificence and just zip down into the ocean to meet your family, and I— Are you *laughing* at me?"

"No!" At her look, he relented. "Okay, maybe a little."

"Thanks a lot."

"It's not that I find it funny, so much as…I was expecting something terrible. You just made it sound so dire."

"Isn't it?"

"It's a hell of a lot more manageable than, say, facing the chance that I'd never be able to be human again, and we'd have to carve out a relationship around my complete inability to exist in your world."

"I…" Her cheeks flushed with embarrassment. "Yeah, when you put it that way, I guess you're right. But I don't want you to…"

"Not want you anymore?" He took her hands again. "My darling Opal, that's simply not possible."

She released a small laugh, and he captured it with his lips.

"I only made the necklace as an option," he continued. "If you never put it on, I'd be perfectly happy. But if you did want to try, I could teach you to swim." He shrugged nonchalantly. "This…*god* —is that how you put it?—is a bit of an expert."

Her laugh was stronger this time. "So I've seen. But I'm pretty hopeless. Can't even float, remember?"

He chuckled, bringing her hands to the gills on his neck. "These help tremendously. They're not just for pleasuring you senseless, you know."

"Huh." A new, highly tempting idea melted her arguments further. "And with both of us underwater, I could inflict a little senselessness of my own, couldn't I?"

Adrian pulled her closer with a sly grin. "I have no doubt in your abilities."

She sighed, leaning into him. "Oh, Adrian. I love you so very much."

"I love you too, my darling."

Opal sank into his kiss once more. Hardly believing the magic around her, happier than she'd ever imagined. Ready to begin a whole new adventure, with the sea creature of her dreams by her side.

Epilogue

A few months later…

"$\mathcal{I}$'ve got your other tuxedo stashed in the trunk. It's ready to go anytime, if you change your mind."

"Opal, relax. Everything's going to be fine." Adrian took his darling's hand. "Need I remind you, this was your idea in the first place?"

Opal scoffed. "Yeah, as an excuse to get you off the lot in a pinch." She gestured out the car window. "Now that you're actually following through with it, it's a bit more nerve-wracking than I expected." She chuckled ruefully. "I just want you to have fun tonight."

"Oh, I think I will. *We* will." He lifted her hand to his lips. "Thank you, love."

She nodded, before leaning in conspiratorially. "Seriously, though, just say the word and I'll send the driver back out for your suit."

Adrian snorted. "I appreciate that. But really. Ms. Reynolds was so kind, and she and everyone else in wardrobe worked awfully hard to make this new tux in time. The least I can do is spend the whole evening in it."

Opal's appreciative smile warmed him through. "You're really something, you know that?" She kissed his cheek, then turned to look out the window again.

Their limousine finally reached the front of the line. Outside, the red carpet-lined street was illuminated by the blazing theater marquee. The popping of flashbulbs punctuated the chatter from the reporters gathered for the premiere of *The Kelp-Dweller from Fathoms Below*.

Opal paused before reaching for the door handle. "You ready?"

"Have I mentioned yet how beautiful you look tonight?"

She truly did. The flames of her hair were twisted into a pile of curls atop her head, and she wore his favorite shade of dark red on her lips. Her dress was a slinky, silver-gray creation that clung to her curves in all the right places, decorated with sprinkles of iridescent amethyst crystals which, he was gratified to notice, matched his eyes almost exactly.

"You have," she answered with a smirk—and a blush. "Several times."

"All right, then. I'm ready."

She shook her head in amusement.

Opal exited the vehicle first, stepping aside immediately to give him room. He drew in a deep breath. *Here goes.*

Adrian emerged from the limo. A few gasps sounded before a hush fell over the crowd, time suspending itself for a charged moment.

It wasn't every day one saw a sea creature arrive to a movie premiere in a tuxedo, after all.

He adjusted his jacket and flashed the assemblage a grin. A few titters began, and he decided to lean in and ride the wave. He lifted a webbed hand to pat his cheek, projecting his voice.

"Oh. Do I have something on my face?"

Genuine laughter echoed now, the reporters relaxing into the "publicity stunt" playing out before them. He caught a few murmurings of "clever" and "oh, that's fun" from the group, and sensed Opal's relief as she stood at his side.

He held his arm out to her, and together they made quite a pair. Her dress coordinated with his self even more magically under the lights. Before he knew it, they had worked the entire line of interviewers. He sufficiently charmed the press—and of course, threw in as many references to Opal's brilliance as a designer as possible.

After shaking yet more hands in the lobby, they finally reached their seats. As the lights dimmed for the film, Adrian allowed himself a sigh of relief. This evening was proceeding even better than he'd expected.

His earlier assurances to Opal had been mostly true, though he had been trying to convince a small, nervous part of himself as well. This might be his only opportunity to appear in public as "himself" and he wanted to make the most of it. The fact that everyone at the studio had been so supportive of their somewhat wild publicity idea, especially given their new boss's need to prove herself, meant the world to him.

Luckily, it was going off without a hitch. And so he settled in, Opal's fingers snugly entwined with his, ready to see how the movie had turned out. The response to early cuts had been largely glowing, so he kept his fingers mentally crossed that the public agreed.

He had high hopes, having already hatched a plan. If the film's reception was positive enough, he had a proposition in mind for a sequel, or perhaps even an ongoing project with the studio's fledgling foray into television. As much as he wanted to continue donning other people's shoes as an actor, playing a version of himself from time to time would be a welcome diversion as well.

Adrian had settled into a satisfying balance between both sides of himself. And while his relationship with his parents was still a work in progress, the thought of paying homage to his family, to all of his kind, felt gratifying.

Plus, more screen time as a kelpie would give Opal the chance to revise her earlier design, and add that tattoo she loved so much. He grinned at the thought.

Making her happy was his favorite part of their new world.

MUCH LATER THAT NIGHT, their driver dropped them off at Opal's, or rather their, cottage. He dropped his jacket, along with his extra tux—which he had not, in fact, needed—on the couch and toed off his extra-large shoes.

"That went even better than I dreamed it would," she breathed excitedly.

"It really did."

He pulled open his bowtie as he watched Opal slip out of her silvery heels, and was just about to draw her in for a kiss when she grabbed his hand and tugged him back outside.

"Come on," she commanded with a sly smile.

"Okay." Honestly, he'd follow her anywhere. But that smile intrigued him.

Opal guided them across the deserted beach to their favorite spot, now bathed in moonlight. She let go of his hand and turned to prop one foot up on their rock. Adrian's breath hitched as she lifted her skirt to unclip her stocking and slide it down.

"You know," she said as she worked, "there's something I've always wanted to do." She switched legs. "I told myself I would if I ever got around to learning how to swim."

Now finished, she turned to face him fully. Her dark eyes took on an ethereal cast in the glow reflecting off the water, the hot intent in her gaze incinerating him.

"And now that I've had some lessons from a very talented teacher..."

His voice emerged as a low rumble. "What did you promise yourself?"

Her lips curved seductively. "A midnight skinny dip."

He hissed through his gills, his cock painfully hard in his trousers now.

Opal held his gaze as she reached up to unclasp the halter behind her neck, letting the straps slide down while she tugged the side-zipper at an agonizingly slow pace. She eased the fabric over her hips, careful to keep it largely out of the sand as she stepped out of it and tossed it on the rock with her stockings.

Adrian didn't dare move as he watched her unhook her brassiere. Her eyes still hadn't left his when her tap pants joined the rest of the pile. He was well acquainted with her gorgeous body, but the sight of her, bathed in silver light, robbed him of breath.

"Care to join me?" she purred.

"Always."

He worked through the buttons on his shirt with lightning speed, his pants coming off even faster. She stepped closer, running her hand possessively down his chest. She barely gave him time to savor her touch before she took his hand and pulled him into a run beside her.

The two of them splashed away from the shore, following the trail of the moon into slightly deeper water. The minute their feet left the sand, Adrian's patience ran out.

He pulled her tight against him and kissed her with a groan. Opal wound her arms around his neck and slanted her mouth to deepen the kiss. Before long, her legs circled his hips, and he filled his hands with the perfect curves of her ass. She moaned at the contact, and he swallowed the sound with a chuckle of his own.

"I hope my little otter buddy is already tucked in for the night," he whispered against her neck.

"Oh? Why's that?" He could hear the smile in her voice.

"Because these waters are about to get very indecent." He punctuated this with a slow lick against her pulse, and she shivered in response.

Opal recovered enough to pull back with an arched eyebrow. "About to?"

He grinned. "Okay, *more* indecent."

They laughed together as he guided his cock to her entrance, but the minute she sank down on him, they both hissed.

"Gods, darling. You feel so good." One slow slide, and then he thrust back home. "Every damn time."

She hummed her agreement, undulating her perfect hips against his.

They found their rhythm, keeping time with the waves surrounding them, giving themselves over to each other. Pouring every ounce of their love into one another. They chased their release, him following only seconds behind her, the intensity of it somehow taking them both by surprise.

Perhaps it was being in the water. Perhaps it was simply the perfect end to a perfect night. Whatever it was, Adrian knew without a doubt he'd found his home in Opal. He grinned to himself.

"What?" she asked breathlessly.

"That's true love's fuck indeed."

She threw her head back on a laugh, the sound echoing off the waves and filling his overflowing heart.

Acknowledgments

First of all, thank *you* for reading. This novella was a bit of a departure for me—I may have stayed in Golden-Age Hollywood, but this was my first dip into the monster romance waters, so thanks for diving in with me! My intention was to have some fun with it, and I indeed found lots of joy crafting Opal and Adrian's magical love story. I hope you enjoyed their journey…and all my nods to classic monster flicks and a certain cartoon mermaid's tale!

As whimsical as this story is, part of it did spring from a tiny kernel of fact. Opal's professional arc was not a unique experience for women at this time. If you'd like to dive deeper, you might be interested in Mallory O'Meara's *The Lady from the Black Lagoon*, about real-life animator and makeup artist Milicent Patrick, who was not given proper credit for much of her brilliant work until decades after the fact. While I doubt Milicent encountered any *actual* sea monsters during her lifetime, she and Opal do have in common their struggle with the monstrous patriarchal system in Hollywood.

When it comes to my work, I owe a huge amount to my amazing writing group, my fellow Sploosh Sisters. Amanda Pereira, Jillian Graves, Daria Vernon, and Genevieve Kersten—thank you for your inspiration and friendship. You are all the best, and you manage to make even the dreaded blurb-writing process a little less painful.

A special thank you to Carla, Amanda, and Jillian, for your incredibly helpful beta feedback on the early full draft of this novella—and your comments that not only helped me fine-tune it, but made me laugh right out loud too.

My editor, Michele Chiappetta, once again helped me so much in polishing my writing. Thank you for all your insights and encouragement, and answers to my many questions.

I am tremendously grateful to artist Yulia Yemelianova for the gorgeous illustration gracing the cover of this book. You simply and perfectly captured the feel of Opal and Adrian's love story, and brought their very different hands to life! And thanks again to Daybed Books for the overall cover design, especially that fantastic watery font action that nails the fun vibes of this book.

I need to give a shout-out to Angela James for the Pizza for Pages challenge she started this past summer. Most of this novella was written during the challenge, so thank you for providing that extra push I needed, along with reminders to have fun with it!

As always, my gratitude to all the friends and family who have been so incredibly supportive of my writing journey. It truly means so much to me.

And of course, eternal thanks to my parents for shaping me into the storyteller I am, and always encouraging me to follow my dreams. Your love is woven through every word I put out in the world.

Also by Brianne Gillen

The Phoenix Pictures Series:

DIFFICULT

SINGLE INDEMNITY

A KISS TO BUILD A GRUDGE ON — Coming in 2023!

First Harvest of Love: A Lughnasadh Short Story —
part of the FLAMES, FLIRTS & FESTIVALS anthology

From the Phoenix Pictures Vault:

SEA CREATURES PREFER REDHEADS (a novella)

***

Did you enjoy this book? Please consider leaving a review!

…on Goodreads, Bookbub, or your retailer of choice

About the Author

Brianne Gillen is a romance author, costume designer, theatre educator, and life-long storyteller, based in the Los Angeles area. She loves classic films, especially the screwball comedies of the '30s and '40s, and will never turn down the opportunity to browse the treasure troves otherwise known as vintage clothing stores. She is also a voracious reader and firm believer in happily-ever-afters. She has done a bit of playwriting, and in recent years, has contributed her opinions to a few online publications centering on the art and craft of costume design. Her Phoenix Pictures Series centers around fierce dames and cinnamon-roll gents finding love in late-1940s Hollywood.

For news, updates, & sneak peeks, sign up for Brianne's Newsletter at:

www.briannegillen.com

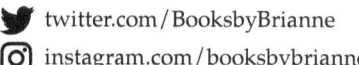 twitter.com/BooksbyBrianne
instagram.com/booksbybrianne